Man On
The Black Jack Gentlemen
Book 4
By Liz Crowe

MAN ON

First edition. May 6, 2024.

Copyright © 2024 Liz Crowe.

ISBN: 979-8223551843

Written by Liz Crowe.

Chapter One

Nicolas stared out the airplane window as the last view of his beloved Valencia faded beneath him. As he shifted in his seat to accommodate his extra-long legs, he accidentally knocked into his seatmate, a striking brunette woman who shot him a nasty glare before doing a double take and switching into recognition-slash-flirtation mode.

She'd obviously flunked Body Language 101. Her attempt to give him a nice cleavage view despite his clear signals to leave him the hell alone grated on his frayed nerves. He clenched his eyes shut, determined to make it all the way to the States without speaking a word to anyone.

The plane shuddered and made terrifying noises as it rose into the air. He nearly leapt out of his skin at the touch of her palm on his unknowingly white-knuckled grip of the seat arm. But he gave her a weak smile and forced himself to relax. Running a hand over his days-old stubble, he took a breath and closed his eyes again, praying the sheer force of his will could maintain the aircraft's ability to stay aloft.

Nicco hated flying. He had gotten used to it as a member of three different European football teams and, for one brief shining moment, the Spanish national team. But he never enjoyed it.

"Whew." the woman sighed and stretched her arms out, bumping up against his shoulder. No accident, he knew. "Glad that part's over." Her accent screamed American. Her chic dark suit, perfect hair and makeup were equally as loud screaming "money."

"Huh," he grunted and stuck ear buds in his ears in an effort to ward off any further conversational gambits, not in the mood for flirting, explanations, or small talk. He was Nicolas Garza, former star attacking midfielder for Real Madrid, Deportivo, and most recently Valencia. And now he was well on his way to utter soccer ignominy as part of a startup team in the United States, in bloody Detroit of all places. He firmly believed that he'd been forced into retirement and resented every cocky asshole of a rising superstar who'd jostled him out of his position.

Harsh rap music filled the space between his ears as he gazed out into the increasingly blue sky. Nicco pressed his aching forehead against the small window. Images rushed at him, jumbled, like a movie stuck on fast forward. Voices he never wanted to hear again berated him, still.

His agent, his ex-wife, his own mother, all of them yelling at him in various stages of pissed off at his seeming inability to control himself, to stay out of trouble. Nicco winced, recalling the exact moment his big-time agent handed him over to one of the agency minions with a disapproving frown. Which hurt way worse than the moment the lovely, expensive, ex-Mrs. Garza heaved an empty wine bottle at him, nailing him in the temple, then stomping out yelling curses and promises about her attorney and alimony.

He sighed and kept staring out the window. She'd made good on all of it, but he was shed of her, which was better for them both.

Nicco closed his eyes and let the curse-riddled rap shove out the one voice he wanted to hear so badly he could feel it deep in his gut, like an insatiable hunger. A memory floated across his unsuspecting brain, making him gasp and clench his hands into fists. A dark face, handsome beyond imagining, soft full lips, an impish smile and sparkling deep brown eyes—the complete package of his beloved, sexy, Leandro. The man who'd proven to him what it meant to feel, to go beyond the raw physicality of sex and connect on a deeper level.

"Shit," he muttered, a familiar burn firing up behind his eyes. He pressed his fingertips to the bridge of his nose as agony bloomed in his chest.

They'd been together nearly eight months. Nicco had been ready to come out, to claim the truth of their relationship in public, while Leandro cautioned against it. They were both highly paid European soccer stars in the spotlight. Despite attitude advances in some pro sports regarding non-heterosexual team members, soccer seemed to be the last bastion of homophobia.

Before Leandro had burst into his world, Nicco rarely turned down a new experience, and one of his favorite positions was between a lovely, sexy woman and the hard, lean muscular body of a man. No big deal, he'd thought. It was his business how and with whom he got off. But the experience of opening himself up to Leandro and his desire to shout it to the rooftops had proven him wrong about that.

The plane bumped, jouncing Nicco's head against the window and sending a fresh jolt of visceral terror down his spine. But at least Leandro's face was forced out of his mind for a brief moment. He bent over his knees, determined not to panic and leap up to pace the aisle, or puke. But both felt imminent. So he focused downward, saying his Hail Marys in preparation for the imminent and inevitable plummet into the ocean.

The girl he'd been ignoring touched his shoulder. "You okay? Want some water?"

Her hand dropped to his thigh. He stared at its well-manicured tastefulness, complete with a wide silver band on her left ring finger. His gaze traveled up her bare, toned arm, followed the slim line of her neck to her jaw and lingered over her full lips.

He'd do anything to ease the knot of frustrated anger in his chest. Besides, sex relieved his stress—it was a well-known fact and something he'd embraced as a much younger man. He'd actually pondered seeing a professional about his near constant requirement for physical connection.

What the hell. Why not?

He allowed a smile to light his face and covered her hand with his, giving it a squeeze, shifting so her fingers slipped a bit further down the inside of his thigh. His body tingled in a distracting way, bringing a hint of legitimacy to his grin. She met it halfway and tugged the blanket she'd had tucked around her bare knees across his lap. He lifted the armrest between them up and out of the way never removing his gaze from hers.

Stop, Nicco. Remember you were going to leave this behind. All the random hookups and bullshit that ruined your marriage and your relationship with Leandro.

Ironically, it had been his ex-wife who'd broken the news flash to the panting press. Nicco Garza was *maricon, el homosexual,* and had been for years. Nicco shook his head at the memory of her flawless body, perfect face, and evil mind. The damn woman had participated in her fair share of three-ways with him and women and other men.

Jesu save him from hypocritical, jealous, vindictive women. But no one had saved him. His reputation suffered a near fatal blow once she figured out that Leandro, a member of a rival team, ten years younger than Nicco, had captured his heart, shoving her out of the picture for good.

His agent had been stoic at first, taking it in stride. Nicco had always been fodder for the gossip-mongering press corps following European soccer players' every move both on and off the pitch. He was tall, handsome, scary talented, and knew his way around the party scene as well as he did around the pitch.

He'd managed to keep his main obsession a secret, or so he thought. Gay players in soccer were simply not tolerated. He understood that. He also knew at least a dozen players between England, Germany, South America, and Spain who held their own secrets close to their hearts. Of course, he would be the one to be a pace setter, thanks to his jealous ex-wife.

Ghostly images of all the men and women who'd paraded through his life and bed lit his brain as he moved close enough to run a finger along his seat mate's knee under the blanket.

"You're nothing but a whore, Nicco. If there's a hole, your goddamned cock is in it." The last words of the only person he'd every truly loved

echoed in his brain but he shut it out, deciding instead to take a deep breath of feminine perfume—a heady mix of soft citrus and pure, spicy lust. *Screw Leandro. He flew off in a plane that never brought him back. He left me—and he was the one man who quelled my need, who calmed my whole self.*

Fate, they said.

Pilot error, the final report said.

His lips found the woman's neck, briefly quieting the fury that had been building for weeks. The breathy sounds of her satisfaction made music in his ears and the sensation of her soft palm gripping him under the blanket forced the memory of the one face he yearned for, the one voice he dreamed of nightly, up and out of his brain, at least for a few moments.

Wrong, his better self said. *Stop. Don't do this with this total stranger on a plane, under the noses of every other passenger.*

Shut up, his true self retorted. *Fuck off. Who cares? Nobody. That's who. Not anymore.*

Chapter Two

Rafael Inez glared at the man seated across from him, then rose and walked to the single window in his office. Nicolas Garza was a guaranteed pain in everyone's ass from day one. Rafe knew it, but he'd thought it worthwhile since he got to scoop him up on the cheap. But now....

"Look, Garza, do what you want on your own time. We're all adults here."

Nicco glared at the young coach but kept his mouth shut.

"I know what they say about you, and I want you to know that I don't care. You can be a completely out-of-the-closet player on my team. I'll support it in public. The marketing department agrees with me. They even have...um...." Rafe ran a hand through his hair. "Sports Inc. has a crew ready to cover it, to show how open-minded we all are. Or some shit."

Nicco's gaze never wavered from his. His square jaw clenched, which was the only indication Rafe had that the man had even registered his words. He leaned on his desk, staring at the one guy he had hoped would help build his team. Nicco would—could—bring a level of maturity the Black Jacks desperately needed, riddled as they were with raw rookies.

"That's why I'm here? To be your show pony? The bad boy who likes boys but hey, look how cool we are in America. We embrace him. Fuck you, *patron*."

Rafe sighed. Personally, he'd wanted to avoid this wrinkle. But the marketing department practically had an group orgasm when he'd told her he'd gotten Nicco signed.

"Oh god, he's that gay one, isn't he? That is *awesome!*"

Her gang of seeming teenagers that made up the huge promotions department for the team had concocted all sorts of media ops for the guy. Rafe had tried to explain to the woman in charge of them who'd been recruited away from an internet social networking company on the West Coast to run all things marketing for them in Detroit, that getting out in front of the curve on the "gay athlete thing" might not be the best focus during their inaugural season. They had enough to worry about. Bringing the bright light of scrutiny over such a controversial topic made Rafe more than a little uneasy. He had enough to worry about, trying to cobble together a decent team from the rag-tag gang of former super stars and raw rookies.

She'd been allowed to run with it, at least to the point he was now telling Nicco about it. And the conversation was going about as he expected—straight into the shitter. He switched to Spanish, hoping their mutual native tongue could help them work this out.

Rafe tried to keep his voice neutral. "Nicco, I won't do anything you don't want to do with this. Trust me. I'm here to lay it out for you, to see if you're interested in playing poster boy for gay pro athletes. Honestly, I don't think the team needs it this early, before we even play a game." He straightened, remembering why he'd been pissed off at the man already, "But I won't tolerate psychotic groupies hanging around my training sessions."

Nicco raised an eyebrow. His lanky body relaxed, showing no sign of stress over the fact that he had just been asked to do something no pro soccer player who currently played had managed to do: to come out as gay, then simply resume his position on the team as if nothing had happened.

"Seriously, *patron*," Rafe said, getting even more irritated by the man's obtuse stance. He kept going in rapid-fire Spanish. "I don't know who she is or where you picked her up between Spain and Michigan, but tell her if she shows up at this facility again, making a scene trying to get to you, I will call the police. And you, my confusing friend, are back to the farm leagues of Europe. I don't need this distraction, and neither do you. It's immaterial to me what kind of sex you have and with what gender. All I ask is that you keep the crazies away from this place and your teammates. We clear?"

"Ah, the farm leagues." The tall, handsome Spaniard stretched his legs out in front him, not taking the hint that Rafe wanted him out of the office. He spoke in accented English, rebuffing Rafe's linguistic olive branch. "I'm pretty sure that's where I already am. Besides, aren't you just filling in until the real manager is hired?"

Rafe closed his eyes and tried to maintain his cool. "Think whatever you want. I'm telling you right now that this team will be staffed with pros and I expect pro behavior from everyone. While I will tolerate WAGs, I will not put up with some obsessive you picked up on the fucking plane. Got me?"

His high-priced, somewhat over the hill, superstar attacking midfielder stretched his arms over his head and then got to his feet and walked straight into Rafe's personal space.

Typical.

Rafe stood his ground. He'd played against this jerk in a World Cup qualifier, the year before the career-ending injury that landed him alone in the American Midwest. The Black Jacks had deep pockets, thanks to the investors who wanted the "real deal" when it came to this particular sport. He'd been able to sign a lot of American-based rising stars and a handful of European near has-beens like this one. But he'd taken a calculated risk, signing Nicco Garza. He'd be damned if he'd let this fucker intimidate him.

"You don't scare me. And yeah, I'm filling in until I can convince that stubborn Turk to take the job. You know that. Jesus, man, you're the only one in the building who truly gets this. Work with me. I'll keep the marketing whiz kids off your back. I can nix the gay poster boy project. Just tell me now."

The other man's deep brown eyes narrowed. Then he winked and patted Rafe's cheek. "You got it, *patron*." He shouldered past him into the hallway, whistling.

Rafe watched him go, fists clenched in repressed need to hit something. He'd been warned by several men who'd been in his position as Nicco's coach and manager before.

"A rare, raw talent. And a shit of a human being."

"Can't see past the end of his own cock long enough to focus. Otherwise he'd still be world class."

"If you can channel him for the game, you won't lose. If you can't, your life is a guaranteed living hell of scandal, booze, and babysitting his ego."

Rafe knew about Nicco's not-so-secret bisexuality. Understood that his marriage had dissolved when his ex-wife had discovered his affair with a man. A man who'd died along with his entire team when their plane crashed between South America and Australia.

Rafe had done his homework and also realized there were even darker rumors about Nicolas Garza—drinking, drugs, a sex addiction—which could destroy what was once one of the very best soccer athletes in the entire world. It was no wonder the guy's second string agent had jumped at this opportunity. He'd needed a player of Nicco's caliber and experience. Nicco had needed a way out of Europe.

Rafe sincerely hoped that he hadn't opened a giant can of worms bringing the guy into the anti-gay, puritanical arena of American professional sports. How his marketing department honestly believed parading him around like ... like a show pony, as he'd said, bragging about how open-minded the new expansion league and its teams were by respecting their players' personal lives all the way into the bedroom could in any way be a good plan, he had no idea. He groaned and sank into his chair, contemplating the dream roster he had posted on a white board on the wall. What had he been thinking anyway?

Maureen, his wife, had laughed herself into hiccups when he came home and bragged about signing Nicolas Garza to the Detroit Black Jacks. Her teenaged twins, a son and daughter, both hot-shit club players and huge fans of the Euro leagues themselves, asked one question: "Why?"

Rafe hoped they were all wrong. As a bonus to all this drama, he had hit yet another snag in his attempt to get Metin Sevim, former superstar forward in the Spanish premier league a decade before, to agree to come out of early retirement and coach. He was a perfect fit—young, with a defensive, strategic mindset both Rafe and the ownership board agreed was key to their success. If only they could convince the guy to listen to them.

A group of businessmen had spearheaded the effort to get Detroit included in the latest MLS expansion, with his own brother-in-law, Jack Gordon at the helm. It stood to reason. Michigan had a ton of premiere soccer clubs. Its major city had successful pro teams in most other sports already. The money had been conjured thanks to a well-connected board, the D-Town Casino and an auto supply company.

They'd put Rafe in charge of recruiting players and finding a coach. Then hired an incredibly slick marketing department with social networking platforms and regular promotions lined up for the young team already.

Rafe had his doubts about some of the control the front office was given over the players and hoped the team's operations manager knew what he was doing. This whole "Black Jacks embrace same-sex relationships. Signs openly gay player from Spain" thing he was prepared to cut off at the knees. Nicco didn't need it. A team still in its infancy certainly wouldn't benefit from it.

The rest of it he facilitated, heading off the grumbling from players when they were issued their smart phones and laptop computers. They were required by contract to cancel any and all social networking accounts they currently held, then re-open them, using the Black Jacks as their "employer" and posting photos of fellow team members, practices, uniforms, events, anything as long as the updates came twice a day at a minimum, were always positive, preferably referencing the team. Anyone caught with a secret account could be let go according to their signed agreements.

The marketing lady knew her shit. Rafe had been assured. So when her staff caught one or more of the players slacking, cursing on line, complaining, or in any way sounding like they were not one hundred percent enamored to be a part of the Black Jacks and the expansion league, said player got dragged into Rafe's office for a chat about their contractual obligations. He hated it. But he recognized it as part of the new world order. The capture of hearts, minds, and wallets needed to be done via social networking.

He grabbed his overnight case and locked the door behind him. He had tickets to the NCAA Men's championship game in Louisville, Kentucky, and less than an hour to get to the airport and checked in, thanks to his star player's first day of practice melodrama.

A player on the Louisville team, supposedly headed to medical school with no interest in playing professionally, had caught his eye. Rafe had bet his unborn child's first birthday present that Parker Rollings would be a perfect foil for Nicco at midfield and he could build a powerhouse of a team around them. One that might make the league sit up and take notice in the first year. If he could only convince the young man that "soccer" made a better choice than "doctor"—and based on what he'd read between the lines of various interviews with the kid, Rafe believed his chances were good.

Chapter Three

Nicolas glared at the line of soccer balls, blaming them for the shit direction his life had gone. He got a running start at the first of the twenty spheres and drew his right leg back. Relishing the hard, jarring sensation of connection shooting up from his foot through his knee to his hip, he sent it sailing to the top right corner of the empty net.

Maybe if he'd gone in a different direction, not heeded all the stupid ravings about him as a kid.

Wham. Another bull's eye hit.

Maybe if his mother hadn't gotten starry-eyed and greedy, pushing him ever harder on the pitch and away from schoolwork. He grimaced as the one he'd hit with his weak left leg went sailing wide and hit the post. He'd been recruited to *La Liga*, Spain's soccer league, at eighteen and never darkened the door of a university—something he still regretted, leaving him wondering how his life might have turned out.

He grunted and sent another ball straight to the middle of the net, exactly where any decent goalkeeper would catch it. Maybe if he didn't feel so alone, so empty, so bereft of real emotion, he wouldn't seek out near constant physical connections. Maybe he could wake up not so angry every day.

He had hoped this little adventure to America would help. So far, not so much. The girl who'd given him a hand job on the plane was sticking like super glue. Although today he had texted her the coach's warning and hadn't heard from her again. Hopefully she'd gotten the message.

Despite his seeming ability to find it around every corner, trouble didn't make him happy. Especially now, as he tried to manufacture a new persona for himself: Nicolas Garza, the wise old man on the pitch at twenty-nine, coming to the aid of this amusing Detroit soccer project.

His next kick went wild to the left, pissing him off even more.

Maybe if the last words he shared with the love of his life hadn't been furious and full of hurt. He'd wanted to quit soccer for the man, for Leandro, honest to Christ. He had loved him so completely, so fiercely, it terrified him. Which had led to his fatal overreaction in the other direction, moving away from emotion and toward emptiness via more random hookups with strangers. He sat on the grass, chest heaving, holding back tears as night fell over the field.

He stared at his hands, turning them over, marveling at how much trouble they'd gotten him into since his lover had slammed the door on their last argument and boarded a plane. They'd been teammates for Deportivo when they met and damn good ones, but Leandro got traded, placing him opposite Nicco for many games.

Their connection had been instantaneous and intense. Leandro Roberto, or "just Leandro" as is the way of Brazilian footballers, brought out the small bit of good left in Nicco. The guy calmed him, and provided stability in a world of crazed fans, money, parties, and bullshit. But Nicco had screwed up, getting angry with the man for something he couldn't even recall. So he, Nicco, had been coaxed into some villa for an party that was an orgy by the end of it.

He put his head in his hands, and let the cool night air dry the sweat from two hours of running and solitary practice. This stupid, beautiful game represented all he knew, all he understood, all he loved. It brought him ecstasy and misery in equal measure. It had given him Leandro, and had taken him away forever. So now, stuck here in no-man's-land, with a former rival for a manager and a female stalker, he faced his final destiny.

As a bonus, his new team wanted to shove him into the spotlight, framing their open-mindedness by making him the spokesperson for gay athletes. God. What a mess. He sincerely hoped Rafe had gotten his unspoken message. He had no interest in being anyone's poster boy. His sex life was his business and no one else's.

He'd taken perverse pleasure in doing the requisite social networking by writing swear words in Spanish for a while, until he'd gotten caught. Then he used utterly idiotic posts like: "Just took a hot shower. Next time you should join me." Or "I need breakfast. Can some woman come make it for me?" All of which earned him yet more slaps on his wrist—and thousands more followers every day, in a perverse counter-reaction to the marketing department's efforts. At the moment Nicco Garza was the most popular team member on the socials.

He leaned back on his hands, taking in the night sky and the huge, hulking indoor venue the team called home next to the grass field he preferred. This Midwest ghost town next to Canada chilled him. He hated it. But he had no choice. He had nothing really but his game.

And his next fuck.

He got to his feet, forcing emotion out of his head, gathered the balls and lined them up again.

• • • •

NICCO WOKE WITH A START and sat straight up in the bed as the hangover grabbed his brain in a pair of steel vise grips. Looking down at the jumble of arms and legs in the king-sized bed he groaned and tried to disentangle himself. Once the room stopped spinning, he sat back against the silken duvet cover.

The pile of flesh on the bed moved, grunted, and rolled over, revealing a man, his deep brown skin as firm as only the truly young can boast. Nicco's body reacted to it as snippets from the night before raced through his consciousness.

He rose and dropped a blanket over the guy, his requirement for hydration way stronger than his need to get laid again. By the time he'd downed three bottles of water in the kitchen, the attractive man was behind him, kissing his shoulders, pressing against him in a way that made him grin.

He arched his back and tugged open a drawer to grab another condom. The pleasant buzz of physical need drowned out the reminders that, if the sting in his ass was correct, he'd done this more than once in the past twenty-four hours. The pain of repeated contact was overpowered by the sensation of the man's hand on his flesh, of his lips on Nicco's greedy skin. He gasped in pleasure when the man spun him around and pulled him close for a tongue-tangling kiss.

He broke away, staring into the perfect stranger's eyes.

"I want you to fuck me this time, soccer boy," the man growled. Nicco smiled and took the condom, grunting in surprise when a completely naked woman appeared, sleep-scruffy and gorgeous.

Ah, Nicco. He sighed to himself before succumbing to their efforts. *You truly are a goddamned mess.*

Chapter Four

Parker groaned and rolled his shoulders. As his teammates' voices filled the outer hallway, he had to grip the open locker door to keep from dropping into a crouch in an attempt to escape the pain in his skull.

Just one more game—one more match, and his life as soccer player would come to an end. He shut his eyes so he could focus on not throwing up. The rest of the team burst into the room, slapping asses, joking and tugging off practice uniforms. He sat, trying to remain calm.

"Yo, Doc, you okay?" He shrugged the hand off his shoulder and pulled his soaking wet practice shirt off before grabbing a towel and heading to the showers. His neck ached from the blow he'd taken winning a fifty-fifty ball during a scrimmage. A random, unintended elbow from a teammate had bestowed a massive nosebleed and likely double black eye on him in the process.

He didn't trust his voice at the moment, especially since stars were dancing around the edges of his vision. He'd blown the trainer off, put ice on his swollen face and sat watching the rest of the practice—their last before the NCAA final game to be played on their home field tomorrow afternoon.

The other men swarmed the showers, forcing Parker to hang onto the edge of the door to keep his balance. He swayed, hoping no one would notice. He knew damn good and well he had a concussion but was not about to let on and lose his starting spot.

The swirl of steam, soap, and chiseled male bodies did its usual song and dance on his nerve endings. Reverting to his standard comfort zone, he made himself picture his girlfriend Christie, her soft hair and deep blue eyes. The way she'd eased him into a sexual relationship within a few weeks of meeting him at college almost without his noticing still shocked him.

He wasn't complaining, although her overall hyper organization leached over into other aspects of their relationship enough to make him deeply unhappy with his own complacency.

"Doc! Toss me the shampoo!" He opened his eyes without realizing he'd closed them and came face to face with Jax—Jackson Reynolds, their star goalie, already recruited and signed to play for Manchester United after graduation and hands down the most well-endowed male on the planet.

Grinning as he rubbed soap down his well-cut torso, Jax held out a hand for the bottle Parker tossed his way. For a split second, unable to could stop himself, Parker saw his teammate fist his amazingly long cock, ostensibly cleaning himself but with an enthusiasm that made Parker breathless.

"Fucking-A Excalibur, spare us the whack-off session, would ya?" a voice called through the thickening steam. "We all know how much you love yourself. But we don't wanna watch."

Jax flipped off the room in general and turned back around to face the water, much to Parker's relief.

"Hey Doc," their trainer's voice broke through the general bullshit eddying around the shower room. "Come see me when you're done." Parker put a hand on the tiled wall. He refused to jeopardize his chance to start in the last game of his soccer career. But he couldn't fake not having a concussion much longer.

He cleaned up, toweled off, and tugged on jeans and a team sweatshirt, ignoring the near constant pounding behind his eyes and the regular stream of texts from Christie.

He sat, gulped down more water, and pulled the final acceptance letter from the University of Michigan School of Medicine from his backpack. Finally, his father's dream fulfilled. Wincing at the thought of the dinner his parents had planned for him and Christie the night after the NCAA championship game—and the not so subtle expectation that he produce an engagement ring for her—he stared at his locker, his number, name, and captain's arm band.

Blaming the tears pressing behind his eyes on the blow to the head, he turned away from it all. Nearly nineteen years of his life had been devoted to playing the sport he adored. Practices, club politics, high school roughness, state championships, and snagging a scholarship position on the University of Louisville's top ranked team—all done now. He'd never play again. Nausea clogged his throat at the thought.

He could play at the next level, maybe even in Europe. But Dr. and Mrs. Rollings had other plans for their only child, ones that included the letters "M.D.", the lovely blonde college sweetheart wife, suburban house, and two point five similarly blonde-haired, blue-eyed children. He shuddered and made his way into the trainer's office, an "I'm okay" smile plastered to his face.

Something he'd long suspected about his own sexuality made his intimate moments with Christie a struggle lately. His body would cooperate. He had little problem getting hard, staying that way, pleasuring her. But it held little appeal for him. She was simply not what he wanted.

Parker Rollings was a good boy, an obedient young man who did not rock boats or upset apple carts. His tyrannical father and heavy-handed mother had only the one son, their golden boy. They had poured years of double-focused energy into molding Parker into the man they wanted—with the M.D., the wife, the kids.

So he accommodated them, thinking nothing more than to please those who loved him with such ferocity. Until now—because he wanted to play soccer, not go to medical school. He wanted it so deeply it hurt his gut and kept him up at night. That, and the fact that he very much wanted to have sex with a man to see if what he suspected about himself was true.

. . . .

PARKER GLANCED AROUND the field as the game kicked off, checking in with his various teammates using the non-verbal cues they'd invented years ago. Nervous energy buzzed through his brain, which remained fuzzy even with a double hit of Tylenol and a solid ten hours of sleep the night before. He'd begged off Christie's requests for dinner, and after finalizing a paper for his last class he'd fallen face first on the bed and passed out for the better part of the night, rising only to drink more water and take another pain killer.

The match commenced. Within minutes Parker realized he couldn't—shouldn't—play. His presence in his current state wasn't helping. It was, in fact, a detriment. He would make mistakes and cost his team this crucial game.

Gritting his teeth against a near constant hum of nausea and pain, he moved the ball around, passed it off when he should have taken shots, ignoring ongoing commentary from the sidelines. As his own teammates kept yelling at him, he lost his usual ability to manage the field, which left teammates floundering and playing kick ball instead of the level of soccer that got them to the collegiate championship game in the first place.

"Nice try, loser." The opposing player slammed into him and stole the ball with a move Parker had learned how to thwart in middle school. "Now get out of my way." The yellow-uniformed player eased past Parker's defenders, nailing the ball square into the upper right of the goal. A groan rose from the sold-out crowd, but he remained frozen in place.

Trained to take a full ninety minutes or more of constant running and contact, Parker dreaded the inevitable request for a substitute. He loved this damn game. Had loved it his whole life. The combination of a concussion and the emotion at over leaving the field on this, his final game, almost brought him to his knees.

He persevered through halftime, redeeming himself at the thirty-fifth minute of play with a strategic shift to the left and a feed to his forward, which drew the defenders off goal, allowing him to take the return pass and plant the ball in the back of the net.

The resulting congratulatory scrum almost made him pass out, but he kept on, and at the break the score remained one-one. He gulped down Gatorade and tried not to meet his coach's eyes.

"Goddammit, Doc." The man materialized in front of him, ending the little charade. "Where the hell is your head?" The trainer eased the coach aside and knelt in front of him, holding out a singlet indicating his ass would be planted for the start of the second half.

"No way. I need him in there." The coach sputtered and complained, but lost the battle to the older man who had a thriving orthopedics practice, a lifelong love for soccer and took his role of team medical advisor seriously. He put a hand on Parker's shoulder.

"He sits, or he risks brain injury." The coach slunk off, shooting an eye full of evil at the kid who'd popped his star midfielder in the noggin during yesterday's scrimmage. Parker leaned back and took deep breaths, trying to keep his last meal down.

The team readied itself and took the field again while Parker watched from a completely unique perspective on the sidelines. He'd been a starter from the get-go and his stomach roiled with the additional misery of having to sit this one out.

At the eighty-second minute of play he stood and started pacing, calling out instructions based on how he observed the other team shifting to adjust to his team's pace. He watched in horror as Chris Singleton, their star forward, who was headed for the English Premiere league, went up to head in a goal and a defender came out of nowhere, undercutting him and forcing the man to land funny, buckling an ankle in sickening slow motion. Parker yanked off his singlet and stood, staring at the trainer and coach, daring them to say no. Since he'd been pulled for an injury evaluation, he could get subbed back in, per NCAA rules.

Taking their silence for agreement, he rushed out, slapping a high five to Chris as he was helped off the field. The scoreboard told the story. He had exactly three minutes to end this thing or risk overtime. His team wouldn't fare well past ninety minutes into penalty play. They were gassed and needed to finish this off now.

Calling out a few quick changes, he repositioned his defenders four back, and shoved a forward to mid so he could set up a play they'd worked on for the last six weeks, with himself in scoring position.

The men readjusted without comment, and the whistle blew. The re-aligned midfield took control, passing and keeping the ball away from the other team's aggressive forwards long enough to draw the opposing defenders into the fray at the center of the field. He made his way across the front of the goal and lifted a hand as the clock ticked towards ninety minutes. Accepting the long pass, he faked to his right then nailed it with his left foot, planting the ball firmly in the back left corner as the horn sounded, signaling the end of the game.

• • • •

RAFE ROSE, SMILING as the Cardinal fans took the field, swarming over their team and its star captain, Parker Rollings. He made his way down to the pitch after a few minutes and tapped the coach on the shoulder, flashing his credentials.

Soaked from a cooler full of Gatorade, the coach followed Rafe to the other side of the field. Several other MLS scouts and even one from La Liga were lurking around, but Rafe's own star power as a former World Cup level player and the amount of hype the marketing department had pumped out about his team gave him the entrée he needed.

The two men sat on the empty bench and observed the celebrations. "So I assume you're here about Parker. He's one of my only players not signed."

"Yes, I am. Can I talk to him?"

"Sure. I mean, officially. But he won't go. He's already turned down bigger names than yours. He's done with soccer after today, at least as a player."

"Something tells me after this game he might change his tune." Rafe used a confident tone, hoping to convince the coach to help him.

"Good luck. He's a quiet kid. Super smart and talented, as you and many others realize. A waste of a great player if you ask me. But he's bound by what his parents want, and they want a doctor, not a professional athlete in the family." The coach shook his head. "If you can convince him to play for your start-up team, you'll not only be the envy of every American scout and several European ones, you will make my damn day. Now if you'll excuse me, I gotta go celebrate. I'll send Parker over."

• • • •

PARKER STARED HARD at his girlfriend of nearly four years and willed her to not be so obtuse. Her huge eyes filled with tears as she kept talking and touching him while he packed his bag.

"Honey, I don't mind. I get it. I...I think you *should* keep playing." He slammed the suitcase shut and looked up at the bare walls of his apartment before whirling around to face her.

"No, Christie, you do mind. You wanted me to go to med school as much as my parents did, so you can spare me the about face." He put his hands on his hips, sorry for his harsh words. The urge to be away from her overwhelmed him to the point he had to grit his teeth not to say something worse. "It's over."

She sucked in a breath. "No, it's not." Crossing her arms, she took a step away. Parker watched as if from miles away as he picked up his suitcase and started for the door.

"I'm sorry, but I do. I'm going to Detroit to play soccer. I'm not going to med school in Ann Arbor. I'm not giving you an engagement ring. Actually, we are breaking up right now." He sucked in a breath and bit down his urge to comfort her and stay put as he gently removed her hand from his arm. "Please, let go. We're through."

"No. Parker. I love you. You love me, I know you do. You're just unhappy and confused." Her sudden self-righteous look made him want to yell and throw something—like his fist—through the drywall. She grabbed for his arm again.

He jerked backwards out of her reach. A montage of their years together ran through his head. The early weeks of awkward flirtation...her thrill at being the girlfriend of the school's soccer star...the other girls who threw themselves at him and her smugness when he rebuffed them...the moment they took the last step beyond heavy petting and the hours since spent exploring each other's bodies. All while an extreme fantasy life played out in his head, dreaming of different sorts of bodies under his hands, of long lean torsos and rough faces against his. He sighed and turned back to her, putting a hand to her cheek.

"This is gonna sound trite but I mean it when I say you deserve better than me. It's not you, I swear it. It really is me. I'm not who you think I am. And I'm so sorry to be this guy...the guy who's hurting you."

"You're exactly who I think you are, Parker. A passive aggressive shithead." She flounced past him and threw open the door. "All those nights we laid in my bed and talked about our future. All the times we...." She bit her lip, and Parker shut his eyes so he wouldn't be tempted to take it all back just for the sake of avoiding this very confrontation.

He hated confrontation. He despised disappointing people. He *had* loved her, in his way. But his new goal shone like a bright beacon of hope—to continue playing soccer away from his parents and girlfriend, despite how well-meaning they might consider themselves. He set his jaw, stayed quiet, and let her have her say.

"Never mind. Go. Play your stupid game on that stupid team. I hate you and hope I never see you again." The last spoken at decibels Parker figured deafened dogs in a three-mile radius. His heart sank in his chest at the sight of her familiar hair, face, body as she glared at him.

"I'm sorry." He kept his voice low, his temper under tight control as always. His upbringing as the only child of strict, boring Presbyterians whose biggest fear was making a scene truly left him no choice. Even on the field he managed to be the star player without a hot-headed tendency to lose it in a fit of emotion. Talented, calm, and strong were three adjectives added to his name.

He was a natural leader, coaches always said, but prone to bouts of introspection—as if that were a bad thing. Never had a single red card and only one yellow warning only because he had yelled at a ref to stop play on behalf of an injured player on the opposite team.

His college sweetheart, the one and only sexual partner of his entire life, despite spirited attempts on the part of many soccer player groupies to change that, stared at him. "You'll be sorry, Parker. You aren't cut out for that kind of life. Those pros, they're gonna rip you to shreds. You...." She let a tear slip down her face. Parker stood still, using all of his willpower not to fold her into his arms, to apologize, and go back to the status quo.

Everything in him he truly believed part and parcel of Parker "Doc" Rollings rebelled at this scene. But for the first time in his life he felt compelled to resist what others expected of him—to reach out for what he wanted.

Being a jerk didn't come naturally. And he felt like a class-A one right now. He'd watched so many of his friends and teammates through the years channel their aggression into asshole behavior against women, but he'd managed to stay above the bullshit, content with Christie.

She turned and left without another word, as panic settled deep in his gut. His family had temporarily disowned him for this bout of rebellion, and he had just cut off his one remaining tie to the life he'd led for the last four years—well, for his whole boring, planned-out destiny, he supposed.

He caught sight of himself in the hall mirror. Tall, dark blond hair and blue eyes, jaw rough from lack of attention these past couple of days, he grimaced at himself. *Happy now, Doc? You just threw away everything you know for this fucking game. Better get the hell up to Detroit and make the best of it.*

He squared his shoulders and walked out into a new reality. The niggling doubt and worry about how he could channel his burgeoning sexual awareness still remained. But he'd made his choice. Being a pro athlete left zero room for being bisexual or gay or whatever he was, and he knew it.

He'd find another girl, get married, and have some kids. There was no longer any other option. In the meantime, this break had to be complete, including the one with Christie. He felt strong but weak at the same time. Sure of himself, yet gut-churning terrified. All of which buoyed him, and made him even more positive about his decision.

Chapter Five

Rafe groaned and rolled over, throwing an arm over the swell of Maureen's stomach. "Jesus, woman, you are gonna kill me."

"Complaining are we, stud muffin?" The beautiful, amazing woman who'd changed his life stretched her long legs and sighed. "I warned you, remember? In spite of my birth control shots, bam, I'm knocked up. Your Latino swimmers are a very determined lot."

"But my love, you are voracious." Rafe propped up on an elbow and ran his finger across her lips. "I mean, more than usual."

"Yep. And it will only get worse." She grinned and grabbed his fingertip between her teeth, then gasped and sat straight up making a bolt of panic hit his brain. He scrambled up beside her.

"What, *querida*, are you okay? Shit, did I hurt you? You kept telling me to go harder. Jesus." He ran a hand through his hair and stared at her, worry gnawing at his gut at the sight of her bright red face.

The smile she shot him as she grabbed his hand and put it against the tight swell of her belly made him temporarily forget how to breathe. The strange, fluttery movement under his palm alarmed him more than anything he'd ever experienced. He jerked his hand away. His wife raised an eyebrow at him, making him feel like a shithead.

"What, did you think I was kidding all this time? Gaining weight for the fun of it? That's your kid in there, Inez. The one you wanted." He stared at her, then put his hand on her stomach again, mesmerized by the activity under his palm. A tear dropped on his hand, surprising him.

"Oh, Maureen, I'm sorry. I didn't mean to."

She shook her head. "I'm an emotional wreck and that's only gonna get worse too, lucky you. But I do love you, Rafe." She held his hand in place as they felt their child move inside her. "This just proves it."

He leaned in to capture her delicious lips, sensed his body stirring to attention again in spite of the workout she'd given him last night and this morning.

. . . .

FEAR SNEAKED BACK INTO his psyche as he sat at the kitchen table, nursing his second espresso.

"Morning." Rafe shifted his attention to the young man who wandered into the kitchen, yawning and rubbing his eyes. "Training today?" Adam, half of a set of twins, was living at home for the summer between his freshman and sophomore years at college, helping coach at a local soccer camp. Adam's sister Ella had opted to intern at a public policy think tank in Washington D.C., making her mother insane with worry.

"Yeah," Adam regarded him a minute in that disconcerting adult way he had. "Got your first team meeting today, right?"

"Uh-huh. You can't come, so don't ask."

"Oh, man." Adam slumped in his seat. "But I wanna meet...."

"You will eventually, but I'm not foisting the family on these guys right off the bat." Rafe put a glass of chocolate milk in front of him. "Your top priority today is to guide a bunch of rowdy ten-year-olds into the light of the beautiful game. Focus on that. Drink your milk."

"Whatever." Adam smiled and chugged a huge glass of the stuff. "Hey, are those the uniforms? Can I see 'em?" He made a beeline for the large brown container near the door.

"Sure, fine. But don't...." The young man looked at him expectantly. But Rafe couldn't think of a single thing he could do to harm the damn things. "Never mind. Have at it." He kept sipping coffee, trying to quell the uneasy jumpiness.

When his phone buzzed he sighed, noting Maureen's brother's name on the screen. "Yeah."

"Good luck today, Coach."

"Thanks. I think. How the hell did you talk me in to this anyway?"

"Her name is Maureen. You married her, and if I'm not mistaken, got her knocked up. That's how."

"Oh, right." He put his cup down and decided to end the conversation before he got even more uptight. Jack expected results. Rafe fully intended to deliver them. But his heart pounded a little too hard for his taste at the moment, and he resented the pressure his brother-in-law put on him. "Well, I need to...."

"Sara wants you guys to come over tomorrow night. Got some kind of a celebration dinner planned. Kids welcome."

"Oh, okay. I'll let Maureen coordinate it. I really gotta...."

"I know. I know. I'm micro-managing. God knows I hear it enough from my beloved spouse. It's just ...now that all the players and pieces of the puzzle are in place and I can back off, I don't want to."

"Tell you what, do me a favor and check in over at the new stadium today if you can. I know you love that shit, and I need to focus on the room full of prima donnas I just hired to play for me—well for Metin, once he shows up. But listen, Jack." Rafe hesitated, unsure how to bring it up. "The thing with Nicco. It's a no-go. He's not interested. I need him to focus, and the team does not need the negative publicity right out of the gate. Can you tell the marketing people to back off about it?"

"Sure thing. And for the record, I almost regret having you step aside as coach, now that I see your rapport with those guys. Also, for the same record, I agree with you about Nicco. The last thing we need is to be a target for homophobic assholes."

Rafe ran a hand through his hair, weighing how he should respond but relieved Jack agreed with him about Nicco. "I appreciate your belief in me, but I'm not qualified to be a manager at this level. I'm better off as his assistant. He'll need a good cop. I have a feeling he'll come in and start bashing heads. And I'll bet you even money most of the old guard we have on the team won't want to listen to him at first."

He ended the call and sat gathering his thoughts. The marketing department had set up a blog designed to look as if it wasn't part of their efforts. It had personal information, photos, and all sorts of crap about every player. The whole thing made Rafe uncomfortable but he bowed to the promotional minds. If they were going to make an impact, break through all the clutter of options people had for their discretionary income and get them to buy tickets and attend matches, they had to be in the spotlight, even if they manufactured it. They had to make romantic heroes out of all the players, and of the team itself.

The project had cost millions, including their Black Jacks stadium, which boasted a brew pub, two coffee shops, and several cocktail bars along with the usual concessions. It also had enough wireless technology embedded so no one would ever lose a signal, no matter how much bandwidth got used. Each seat was encoded so when fans checked in on their social networks they could show themselves via the cameras set into every possible angle with the "Black Jack Check In App" available for all smart phones for free #blackjacks #detroit.

Rafe had spent hours designing the locker room to his specifications along with state of the art training and workout facilities. He'd already put up about two thirds of the team in the JW Marriot in a nearby suburb. Where, thanks to one Nicolas Garza, he already had a huge bill for damages to one room from red wine spills and god knows what else.

The fact that the real coach had yet to show up, which left him to lead this rag-tag group of men into their first season on his own made him as nervous as an inside cat. The added bonus of having accidentally gotten his wife pregnant only made it a thousand times worse.

As he drove he practiced his rah-rah-sis-boom-bah and his hardcore take-no-bullshit speeches, trying them on and discarding them in equal measure. *Fuck it. I'll just tell them my plan and give them their phones, room keys, and uniforms. They're grown men. I don't have to hand-hold them that much, please God.*

When he emerged from his SUV in the baking hot parking lot of the soccer practice facility they currently shared with a bunch of kids and parents until the official opening of the Black Jack stadium, he tugged his hat down and stuck his Ray Bans on, as his pulse revved even higher at the sight of several high-priced convertibles and at least two vintage Jags and a Corvette. He grinned. Men, boys, there wasn't much difference especially among pro athletes. They worked hard and played harder, spending their money on fast moving things that made a lot of noise, looked nice, and made them feel important.

Rafe stopped, realizing he could be describing their automobiles as well as their wives and girlfriends. Because along with every pro sports team came the WAG contingent, trailing drama and distractions at every turn. Thank God Nicco had agreed they should keep a lid on the gay athlete thing. He'd said he would lay low and not draw attention to himself.

As long as Rafe kept the media focused on the team, and not on the fact it boasted a player who, for all intents and purposes, had been ruined overseas when his ex-wife claimed he "was as queer as a three-dollar bill." Squaring his shoulders, he walked in, staying under the radar until he ducked into the conference room he'd reserved. He took a breath, closed the shades from prying eyes, turned and faced his team.

Chapter Six

Nicco narrowed his gaze, keeping his feet propped on the conference room table and generally taking up more than his allotted space. He watched the men mill about, greet each other, and ignore him. He'd been in Detroit for almost a month already, had more or less acclimated to the chilly air in the middle of the summer. He felt pretty good, if a little wobbly from last night's overindulgence.

The whole "Black Jacks Pride" bullshit had gone away, thanks in no small part to Rafe. He smiled, recalling the sort of photos that could have been taken last night in his hotel suite with Terrance—Nicco's new obsession.

Terrance had agreed not to talk. Nicco knew better than to believe him, but he did things to Nicco's body with his that negated his potential as secret-teller. He had no intention of giving any of it up anytime soon. It kept him from thinking about anything relative to Leandro, his own personal misery, the booze he consumed, and the fact he was already an outsider on a team that was about to have its first meeting.

His fingertips grazed a small card in his pocket, making him wince at the memory of his first encounter with the team psychologist. He'd set it up one morning after booting Terry out the door, along with a couple of girls he'd convinced to come by for some playtime. His head had been pounding, not so much from a hangover but shame.

When he had flipped through his expensive-looking orientation packet the words "team psychologist" had leapt out at him as if connected to a hand gripping him by the short hairs. Not a new thing. All teams had one these days. So, sick of his bizarre need for constant physical contact—for fucking, he'd corrected—tired of even glossing over it in his own stupid head, he made the call. In the meantime, he'd enjoyed the workouts with the trainers, the few times he'd scrimmaged around with some of the other players. They'd all been contracted but not obligated to do anything for a month but acclimate to their new surroundings.

Part of the acclimation came with the requisite social networking and attendance at some high-visibility fundraisers—which is where Nicco had hooked up with Terrance, who'd been attending as personal assistant to some politician. He'd also been encouraged to look around for a place to live with the assistance of an eager young real estate agent, an adorable, sexy, young lady whose name he had forgotten within minutes of banging her brains out in an empty mini-mansion.

Par for his course, really.

His first session with the psychologist, an earnest, nerdy-looking guy with square glasses, a cleft chin, and a head of long, thick, brown hair, had been brutal. Nicco had deflected and, to his credit, the shrink had let him front and feint like a dumb ass for a full hour.

Then, just as he was getting up to leave, convinced the whole thing had been a total waste, the guy looked up at him, pinning him with eyes so sharp and clear they made Nicco gasp in spite of himself.

"Nicco," he'd said. "When you're ready to face up to your addiction, I'm here to listen. I know you have a problem with sex. You know you have a problem with sex. I'm glad you made this appointment. Next time, let's make it more useful, shall we? And for your information, I didn't support the concept of putting you out there as poster boy for gay rights or gay athletes."

The man had removed his glasses, staring Nicco down as if he could see into his very soul. "I've been with the same partner, a man I love dearly, for six years. I understand, on a certain level, what you're dealing with." He'd put the glasses back on and glanced down at his tablet computer. "So, when will I see you next?"

Now, Nicco pulled the card from his pocket and stared at the therapist's name and phone number. Without much thought, he ripped it into small pieces as the rest of the new team filed into the

"And Parker will be working with you, Nicco."

Nicco sat up, knocking his water to the floor as Rafe's words got his immediate attention. He stared at the polite hand the kid stuck in his face then over at Rafe. His throat closed up between the proximity of the impossibly handsome teammate and realization of the fact that the vision of masculine perfection he'd lusted after for the last few seconds wanted to take his position on the field.

He leaned back again and ignored his inner polite self. Instead, he smirked, ignored the punk, and turned to face their coach as if suddenly fascinated by what the guy had to say. Parker stood a minute, and Nicco watched his face turn red before he sat in the one empty chair nearest the door.

Rafe passed out new phones for everyone since a local provider was one of their sponsors, and reminded them of their obligation to tweet and post profile updates on Instagram at least three times a day. All shit Nicco already knew. Rafe's hot young lady assistant issued key cards to the ones who'd just arrived, including the kid Nicco studiously ignored but whose presence was making the front of his jeans uncomfortable.

He shifted in his seat, trying to get control of himself, a bizarre combination of anger and lust spinning around his brain. The room rose, and Nicco joined them as they made their way out into the hallway.

A gaggle of kids, parents, and media awaited them, and the team spent about an hour signing soccer balls, slips of paper, jerseys, getting photos taken with camera phones while sport journos watched and recorded their every move. Nicco joined in to prove his ability to schmooze. At one point he caught sight of his new young coach with his arm around a tall, attractive, pregnant woman with coal black hair. Rafe caught his eye and beckoned him over. He finished signing, smiled at some kid's hot mom, then made his way over to them.

"Nicolas Garza, this is Maureen, my wife, and her son, Adam." A dark-skinned teenager next to the stunning woman stuck out a hand.

room. He noted two German players he'd had run-ins with i
Cup play, one famous Nigerian player who must have cost th
a pretty penny, at least three Brits, a Welsh guy or maybe Irish,
South Americans whose dark, intense good looks made him shi
memory.

The handful of fresh-faced American rookies intersperse
group made him feel creaky and dusty with age. Which total
him off.

What was Inez thinking anyway?

He also took careful note that there were at least two per
in the room, definitely two strong players for each spot—ex
He sipped his water bottle and glared at the Germans. Nervous
gnawed at his gut but he kept his face calm. Finally wh
temporary coach showed up and flipped the blinds closed, he

So everyone in the room has to fight for their spot except n
works.

He dropped his feet to the floor at Rafe's pointed gla
propped his elbows on the table prepared to ignore the forth
pep talk. He'd already made plans for the night and wanted
up beforehand. This welcome-to-the-team-guys meeting wou
good a time as any. Letting his thoughts wander to the nightcl
discovered that catered to gay men and promised full discre
made himself stop obsessing over the failed therapy session.

The door clicked open and all eyes landed on the tall, blo
who walked in, backpack on his shoulder, dressed to play. Nicc
tingled at the sight of him—strong torso, long legs, firm jaw
with several days' worth of fuzz. Good Christ but he was a
specimen. Nicco kept his casual stance but startled when t
bright blue eyes and huge white smile landed on him.

He resisted the urge to smile back. Something about him
Nicco uncomfortable, but horny at the same time. He wished he
onto the shrink's business card.

Nicco took it, noting the kid's own club kit and backpack. He took Maureen's hand, kissed it, and eyeballed Rafe.

"Well done, young Rafe. What a vision. How did you rate such beauty?"

Maureen frowned but her eyes sparkled. "Spare me, Nicco. I've heard all about you."

"I have no doubt of that, lovely lady." He gave a short bow. "But may I also say congratulations on the impending joy."

She smiled at him, and he mirrored her, liking her already. He appreciated it when women took no shit from him. He winked at Rafe and made his way back into the teeming throng after nodding at the woman's son, who didn't look that much younger than his mother's new husband.

When he accidentally locked gazes with the blond American usurper, his throat closed up. The man stared at him wide-eyed and innocent, and Nicco had to grip the back of a chair to keep from saying something utterly stupid.

He'd wager his left nut that young Parker had never been with a man, but the sexual energy pouring off him was intoxicating. His fresh, clean good looks spoke of a typical American, upper class upbringing, expensive soccer clubs and college scholarships. The sort of advantages Nicco usually denigrated.

He broke the eye contact and set his jaw. The kid had another think coming if he honestly thought he'd be taking Nicolas Garza's place on the team, no matter how fevered his sudden fantasy over popping the kid's cherry. He ran a hand down his face and swallowed hard. Things had certainly gotten complicated and then some. But he had a focus now—keeping his starting spot ahead of the delectable Parker.

Chapter Seven

Parker smiled, signed jerseys, made random small talk with his new teammates, and tried like hell to ignore the blatant glare coming from the famous Spanish player. The guy had a nerve, ignoring him like that in front of everybody. So far, consensus on the team about Nicolas Garza remained consistent—he was the official bad boy, their token player everyone loved to hate, the old man with more experience playing at the highest possible level than anyone else. Parker didn't think it was a good way to initiate team dynamics, but he wasn't the manager.

So he did his thing. Tweeting, making a few Insta posts under his new profile: Parker Rollings Black Jack, signed more balls and grinned for more pictures. By the time they'd finished the fan scrum his ears were ringing and his stomach growly.

"Hey, Parker, do you have a car?" The dark-skinned Nigerian forward slapped his back. "Need a ride?"

"Uh, sure, um...." Parker tried to remember the man's name.

"Kalu."

"No car yet, Kalu, so that would be great, thanks." In Kalu's huge shiny SUV, they were joined by two Germans and a kid Parker vaguely recalled playing against in college. During the brief trip to the hotel, he learned Aric and his quieter fellow German, Tobias had both given up decent careers in the *Bundesleague* to take a chance on this American experiment.

Tobias was married, but his wife had stayed behind for a year just to hedge their bets. Aric had a girlfriend who'd be joining them in a few months. Kalu kept quiet about his personal life, which Parker respected by staying silent about his own.

The other American, Cole Franklin from Somewhere-who-cares-Ohio kept up a steady monologue about himself, his talents, his various trophies and championships, the many women he'd fucked, and how much more pussy he anticipated getting now that he was a pro player, precluding any other conversation.

Parker stared straight ahead listening to the chatter from the back dominated by the loud American and various grunts and one-syllable answers from the Germans. A hard reality struck him then—the gamble he'd taken coming here matched the huge crap shoot nature of the whole project. He had felt such an affinity for Rafe when he'd met him after the championship game, but until that moment he had no idea how far out on a limb he stood with this motley crew of players.

He grinned and looked at Kalu who returned a wide, genuine smile. Maybe it would be fun, he thought. A convertible raced by them, top down, long blonde female hair whipping around on the passenger's side. Parker bit his lip at the sight of Nicolas Garza behind the wheel, one hand draped over it, the other along the back of the seat, his dark face casual as if the whole driving thing was an afterthought.

Swallowing the urge to grip his thighs and clamping down on forbidden fantasy images, he took a long breath. The car sped up and zoomed around them, disappearing into the shimmering heat of the highway ahead.

All his intense imaginings had to remain that—imaginings. He would likely never be able to experience the hard muscular planes of another man's body under his hands. Not if he were to achieve his goal of pro soccer stardom. He swallowed hard and made a mental note to find a girlfriend, fast.

"So Parker. How do you feel about being pitted against Nicco the Terrible?" Kalu asked.

Parker frowned. "Pitted against him? I figured I was just his second."

"Our coach is going old school on us. Making us earn our spots in one-on-one competitions starting on Monday."

Parker's heart sped up. He had always admired the Spaniard's style, but was confident of his own talents. "Huh. Well, I guess I'll have to beat him then." He blushed as the three older men burst out laughing. One of the Germans smacked his shoulder.

"Big talk. You have no idea how hard that bastard will work to keep his spot. But never mind. That's for Monday. It's Thursday and I, for one, have never been in a big American city. I say we hit at least three strip clubs, two casinos, and end the night with an orgy in…your room."

Parker gave a weak grin at the roars of amusement and ran a thumb over the new debit card the pretty, dark-haired assistant had pressed into his hand earlier.

"Plenty of money here, Parker. An advance on your salary to get you settled, per your contract." Parker had never in his life thought much about money. Now on his own, worries about how to actually afford tucking singles into bikini bottoms and throwing cash at the gambling tables invaded his brain.

They pulled into the hotel's swank front court, exited, and made their way to the bank of elevators. Parker's head spun from residual stress, hunger, and anxiety at the thought of an actual strip club. He shook his head.

Get a grip and act like a man, Jesus. Men do these things all the time. No big deal.

He shut the room door and leaned on it a minute, trying to still his racing heart. He'd never regretted his sheltered life as coddled only-son-student-athlete-with-regular-sex-from-a-girlfriend more than at the moment.

He glanced around at the suite, which had both sleeping and sitting areas, plus a luxurious bathroom with a tub and shower big enough to hold a family of six. Parker devoured an apple and a banana from the fruit bowl and tossed his new phone on the marble table top before slumping into a chair and ripping open a packet of almonds.

He stared at the new device wishing he had someone to call. Someone who gave a shit he'd arrived safely and was settling into his new life. But he didn't. His mother had called once leaving a terse, predictable message that made him ache for his old life while at the same time relieved he'd left it behind. He'd made his choice. Although disturbing erotic thoughts of the compelling Spaniard, the guy he was supposed to compete with for his starting position, made him doubt his sanity.

· · · ·

RAFE SIPPED HIS BEER and attempted to relax. Maureen and Adam chattered with one of her friends on either side of him as he smiled at the various locals who stopped at their table to congratulate him on pulling together such a great team. His heart pounded in his ears, the gigantic, colossal mistaken nature of this project whipping through him like a hurricane.

Huge. Epic.

Failure waiting to happen.

His leg bounced from nervousness until Maureen's calm, cool hand touched it. She kept talking to the woman on her right but her palm stroked his thigh, soothing, erotic, and annoying all at once. He wanted to crawl up the damn walls. Why had he put himself in all these simultaneously stressful positions? Jesus, just a year ago, he'd been coaching a group of teenagers on an elite travel team, his main stressors that of parents always pressing for more playing time or positive evaluations for their kids. With no real worries other than where he'd buy his next meal or what girl he would call to take off his edge.

He blinked, and found himself staring at his wife's profile. They had gone through hell to get to this point. It had taken him almost an entire year to convince her he loved her. He wouldn't trade it for a million dollars. Still, he should have taken one glance at her brother's proposal to take on recruiting for this crazy project and said "Hell. No." before running in the opposite direction.

His phone buzzed but he ignored it in favor of easing into Maureen's under-the-table caress, needing her more than he needed anything at the moment. She turned to him, her bright blue eyes comforting. He smiled as the band around his chest loosened an inch or even two.

"Let's go home," she whispered, her hand planted firmly near his crotch, making his scalp zing with anticipation.

"Can't," he whispered back, moving so she could get a better angle. "Jack is coming by. He wants a play by play from the team meeting."

She sighed and sipped her lemonade. "Okay, but it's already nearly nine." She stared at his beer. "Jesus, I wish I could have one of those."

"Hell no, woman. You won't corrupt our son that way."

He leaned into Maureen, taking a deep breath of her scent which had always thrilled him but now had a ripe undercurrent that never failed to bring his whole body to strict attention.

"I love you." He'd never meant anything more sincerely in his life.

She put her head on his shoulder. "I know. And you're going to be fine. This whole thing is going to be great. I know it."

"Yeah, Garza and all, eh?"

"Well, he seemed very nice."

Rafe snorted.

"Realy, he did."

"I hope so. I really really do."

Maureen's brother Jack Gordon dropped into the booth. Maureen leaned over and kissed his cheek. "Hey, handsome."

He ordered a beer, then sat back and unbuttoned his top shirt button. "Fuck me. What a day."

Rafe raised an eyebrow at him.

"Damn market is going haywire. People are back to writing purchase offers on the hood of their agent's cars with promises of cash, more cash, and god knows what just to get the house they want. Like the old days, but Jesus please-us is it stressful." He grinned and sucked back half the amber brew. "Any good news to be had?"

"Well, Sevim gave me a verbal agreement about an hour ago. He'll be in by Friday to sign a contract. Thanks for your help with that." Rafe's personal triumph over signing the Turkish coach faded at the sight of the unfamiliar local number on his phone. He'd programmed in all the players' new numbers so he had no idea who this could be. "Inez," he said into the device.

"Yes, this is the J.W. Marriott. We have a couple of complaints and, um, the noise seems to be coming from your floor. You know, the players' floor."

Rafe groaned. *It starts.*

"All right, I'll call someone on the coaching staff who should be in the building, and I'll be right out."

"Thank you, sir." He hung up and met his brother-in-law's stare. "What? They're grown men."

"You let them loose? Tonight? You do realize where they are right? Smack in the middle of Detroit with casinos, strip bars, and nightclubs in their path?"

He ignored the man's rhetorical question and hit the speed dial for the team manager as he got to his feet. No answer. He ground his teeth and sent a text demanding a return call in the next five minutes.

"A bunch of prima donna professional athletes with too much money and testosterone to blow off. Loose in downtown Detroit. Better call the PR department," Jack said, making Rafe even more irritated. He resisted the urge to snap at the man. Maureen started to slide out of the booth. Rafe took her hand and helped her up.

"I need to get home." She glared at her brother. "You. Be nice." The tension in his face softened as he looked at her.

"I'll update you later," Rafe tossed over his shoulder at Jack as he led her out of the increasingly noisy restaurant. "I'm so sorry." He kissed Maureen's forehead. "I'll be home as soon as I can."

"It'll be fine. The hotel is probably being picky. Go make some threats and get them calmed down. You have training when?"

"Monday." He winced, realizing the mistake, even as he said it.

"Oh, well, um, maybe you should call an impromptu one this weekend—you know, mandatory or something so they don't...I don't know."

As he climbed behind the wheel of his truck and watched Maureen's taillights disappear into the traffic, Rafe tried to figure out how in the hell he'd been named babysitter for a bunch of grown men.

Chapter Eight

The early sun warmed Nicco's skin as he finished the sixth mile of his run. His head had cleared, allowing him into the zone of pain-free euphoria he always reached at about this point every morning. No matter how late he'd been up, what or who he'd been doing, he never, ever, skipped his run.

The fog had burned off a nearby golf course and early players headed to the first hole. The brisk Michigan air brushed across his skin, making him break out in a chill. He slowed, headed up a hill, crested it and stopped, looking around at the vista of bright green. For some reason, it seemed unnatural and surreal, exactly like this entire, American soccer team experiment.

He sighed and started back down the other side, picking up speed and letting the increasing exhaustion in his legs distract him. By the time he got back to the lobby, a bunch of his new teammates had gathered in the coffee shop, jawing and sipping from cardboard cups. They ignored him. He returned the favor, tipping a salute to the hot blonde receptionist who'd given him a stellar blowjob the night before.

Several teammates had made a half-hearted attempt to include him in their lame plans to hit strip clubs and casinos and whatever else Detroit could provide them last night, but he'd demurred and spent the evening between the legs of said lovely behind the desk. A much better tradeoff, considering the young coach had been called in at one point to yell at them all to shut the fuck up or risk getting booted to the curb of the high-class hotel. By the time that happened, he'd been passed out, sated, after sending what's-her-name on her way.

He'd been subjected to a second round with the psychologist and spent a pleasant half our baiting the guy about his own "I'm gay and I'm proud" confession. The he passed the rest of the time staring sullenly at his own shoes.

"See you next week, Nicco," the therapist had said at the quiet end of the hour. Nicco had slammed the door on his way out.

Leaning against the mirrored wall of the elevator, he let endorphins from the hard run rush through his brain. He barely noticed when a hand appeared between the closing doors, forcing them back open. Grimacing at the delay Nicco looked straight into the bright blue eyes of the man who had haunted his wet dreams since he'd clapped eyes on him.

"Oh, um, hi. Sorry." Parker Rollings blushed and ran a nervous hand through his short-cropped blond hair.

Nicco didn't trust his voice so he nodded, annoyed by how his scalp prickled at the young man's proximity. He stood up straighter, letting his gaze traverse the very pleasant landscape of young Parker's, back, waist, and ass. He took a breath, tried to think of something to say but couldn't. Which really pissed him off.

Parker turned to him.

"We got off on the wrong foot."

Nicco nodded, throat closed in agony at the slightly southern cadence of the other man's voice. "So, let's try again." The tall American stuck out a hand. "Hello, I'm Parker Rollings. Pleased to meet you."

Nicco stared at it, willing the muscles and bones of his shoulder and elbow to cooperate. He observed his dark hand gripping Parker's. And just barely resisted the urge to grab the rail behind him at the bright shock of chemistry passing between them.

Parker gasped and yanked his hand back, staring at Nicco as if at a particularly disgusting roadkill. Then, as is the way with polite, well-brought up American boys, he smiled, putting Nicco at ease in way that terrified him and turned him on in equal measure.

"And you are Nicolas Garza, the guy I think I'm supposed to beat if I want my starting spot, correct?" He stood next to Nicco, forcing him to ease away ever so slightly. "Good run?" Nicco's eyes refused to obey his brain's direct orders and stared at the sweat droplets on Parker's shoulders and beautifully defined biceps bead up and disappear in the dry cool air of the small space.

The silence expanded, encompassing Nicco in a cocoon of awkward lust. "Oh, uh, yeah, good run. You?" He passed a shaking hand over his face and moved another few centimeters away from extreme temptation.

The doors slid open. The two men didn't move. Nicco pushed himself away from the wall, his body sore, frozen, old and used. The freshness of the young man pissed him off for some reason. Take his starting spot? Not likely. He fixed what he hoped was a smug look on his face, turned to face Parker's fresh-faced eager youth, and got slammed straight in the libido by a connection so intense his jaw dropped. He clapped his mouth shut and frowned trying to square the warring emotions in his brain.

Yep, time to see that shrink again.

Because something about his frighteningly real reaction to Parker Rollings made him want to whisk the kid away from all of this, somewhere where they could be alone. The young man oozed vulnerability, but it combined with a sort of innate strength just under the surface.

It made every hair on Nicco's body stand up straight. He took a deep breath, started to speak, to say something resembling polite. Something not sounding like *"I want to make love to you until you scream with pleasure."*

Parker spoke first. "Yeah, so see you Monday." Parker put a hand on the back of his neck.

Nicco spoke without thinking. "Some of us are going out tonight. There's this club...."

"Oh, um, I'm not really into...." Parker stopped, seemed to rally himself. "Okay. Great. What time?"

Nicco smiled. *Round one to the old guy.* "Ten-thirty. Meet in the lobby." But he wanted to warn Parker at the same time. To tell him not to come, to avoid it, to avoid him, Nicco, like the plague he was.

"All right, thanks." A smile lit the young man's impossibly handsome face, shooting another bright shaft of desire straight to Nicco's gut. He stepped backward into the hall and lifted a hand at the closing doors then made his slow way to his room, his cock so hard under his loose-fitting shorts it made him limp.

He dropped into a chair, staring out into the sunlight and pondering just what in the hell he would do with young Parker, should he get him alone. Closing his eyes against onrushing emotion, he got up and stumbled into the shower.

• • • •

PARKER STARED AT THE clothes he'd purchased, hoping they'd be okay for the club. Dark jeans, a white shirt with a brown pattern woven around the back and over a shoulder, black shoes with the trendy white soles, new belt, even a new wallet holding more money than he'd ever had on him at one time. His ears buzzed and something zinged his nerve endings he couldn't identify. He ran a hand over his jaw, decided against a shave, and climbed into the shower.

He'd spent nearly three hours practicing trying to work off the nervous energy that kept him buzzing and on edge. About half of the team showed up, and they'd done a few self-directed drills, laughing and getting the measure of each other before the official pre-season team camp started on Monday.

Parker had let his captain's brain take over and observed the group, saw them interact, and allowed the first hint of optimism sneak into his subconscious. This Black Jack thing might work as long as they could pool their collective talents. They were definitely all talented as individuals but it would take a strong personality in the manager's position to turn them into a team.

Parker spent a solid thirty minutes letting hot water wash over him, the lonely space he'd nurtured since getting off the plane from Louisville receding for the first time. The hard workout he'd more or less guided everyone through had helped. His natural leadership tendencies showed themselves in the way the older men deferred to him.

He stood, hands on the cool tile forcing his brain to still, as his body kept revving, sending tingles from his scalp to his toes before settling firmly in his groin. He groaned and turned his fac up to the water, willing it gone.

But the dark eyes and face of the man who would be his nemesis remained bright and compelling. The broad span of his shoulders, trim waist, firm ass and thighs, the memory of the man's lilting Spanish accent filled his consciousness, firing his fevered brain.

He tried to let anger replace the knee-jerk horny. He was not that guy. He was not gay or even bi. He couldn't be. Not and fulfill his dream. He stepped out and dried off, yanking the new clothes on before slapping on some cologne. All in a haze of confused frustration.

A quick memory of Christie, the woman who'd been the first to convince him to wear scent, made him wince. She no longer played a part in his life. He'd left her behind, along with everything else he knew, loved or understood. A great well of loneliness yawned at his feet, making him gulp.

His phone buzzed. He answered as he threaded the new belt through denim loops.

"What's up tonight, Parker?" Kalu had been at the field today, and they'd had a great time with drills and chatter. He remembered now mentioning getting something to eat together later. He winced.

"Oh, ah, I forgot I'm headed out with, um...." He sat, wondering what had possessed him, thinking he could just "go out to a club."

"It's cool. I was just calling to let you know I'm lying low. Drank too much last night, ya know. And you killed me with that workout."

He dropped into a chair suddenly relieved and unsure why. "Sorry. Want to run in the morning?"

"Sure. Behave yourself tonight. Garza will do everything he can to corrupt you."

"How did you...?"

"I just do. Watch yourself, friend."

"I'll be fine. It's just some club."

The other man chuckled, setting Parker's already rattled nerve endings alight. He put the phone down on the table and took a deep breath commanding the vision of the compelling man out of his head for a few more minutes.

Nicco had already summoned a ride for them by the time Parker met up with the five other teammates and an attractive, dark-skinned man he'd never seen before. The steady stream of masculine laughter, commentary on the day's games in Europe, and ribald jokes about the reputation of their interim coach filled the space, allowing Parker time to sit back and observe.

The news that Metin Sevim had been coaxed out of retirement and had agreed to lead them still shocked everyone. Parker knew the guy's back story—everyone who knew soccer did. It was brutal. It truly seemed small miracle he would be showing up within days to coach them.

Nicco dominated the space. He seemed eager to share his vast, deep knowledge of the Euro leagues. Of the other men in the van, only one had played overseas, the rest were rookies like Parker. The dark stranger monopolized Nicco's attention and Parker's eyes fixated on the slender hand he kept on Nicco's thigh.

During the trip to Greektown the men consumed shots of expensive Scotch, which went straight to Parker's head making him wish he he'd eaten something since lunch.

At one point, when the laughter and voices were loudest, Parker glanced over and locked gazes with Nicco. He frowned at the other man's raised eyebrow. What in the hell did he need to prove? Who was that other guy, with his hand on Nicco's leg? Jesus. It all felt contrived, a show for Parker's benefit.

He broke the moment and turned is gaze to the window confused, pissed. The little kid at the grown up party sensation burned a hole in his gut.

"So, Rollings, you got a hot young lady friend joining us out here in the Motor City soon?" The other European older player, Lawrence Williams, a Brit, slapped his shoulder, making Parker flinch at the sudden attention the entire group directed his way. "Surely a strapping handsome lad such as yourself has plenty of opportunity for bird watching before she shows up?"

"Ah, there is no one. At the moment." He took a nervous gulp of his second Scotch. The group laughed louder at his cough as the alcohol burned his throat.

"There's a good lad. No one to disappoint, that's my theory," The guy slammed his drink and leered into Parker's face. "Variety is the spice of life, eh, my fresh-faced American?"

"Bloody virgin if you ask me." The man with the possessive grip on Nicco's thigh smiled into his glass.

"Be nice, Terry." Nicco patted the man's arm then leaned over towards Parker placing a warm palm on his knee. "Don't mind them, love." His lips tickled Parker's ear, lingering over the "love" a little too emphatically for Parker's comfort.

He smiled weakly and sat back, processing how much of a mistake he'd just made, agreeing to accompany this group downtown. Glancing around, he noted all eyes on the awkward scene Nicco had just created.

Nicco's gaze never left his, and for a moment Parker wanted nothing more on the planet than to pull him close, and cover the other man's full lips with his own. He shook his head at himself. This could be a long night.

Chapter Nine

Within thirty minutes of arriving at Club Nubo, on the penthouse level of the D-town Casino, Parker knew he'd made a serious mistake. The huge space, lit only with flashing neon, boasted some of the most beautiful human beings Parker had ever seen in his life. He tried not to gawk to obviously as he sipped a beer and took in the teeming dance floor.

He nearly jumped out of his skin when a barely dressed, model-gorgeous woman touched his arm and ran her hand up his biceps. "New to town, handsome?"

"Uh-huh." Parker's body reacted, but his eyes found Nicco as if pulled by magnets. On the dance floor with what looked like two different women, his lithe, fit body moving in time with theirs, the brutally handsome Spaniard stared right at him.

Parker choked on his beer. The woman stepped away.

"Oh honey, I get you. Sorry." She relaxed. "Have you met my friend, Hugh?" She nodded across the bar to an incredibly tall, thin blond man, who at that moment also stared at him, the bright blue of his eyes piercing and intense. Parker shook his head, still unable to formulate coherent words.

He made a valiant attempt to ignore the way his brain kept pulling him back, kept forcing him to watch Nicco as he moved through the crowd, dancing, groping, kissing. Parker's mouth dried out at the show the man put on, as the music level ramped up ever higher, the loud thump-thump of the bass beating deep in his chest.

He sipped more beer, shoving away his growing uneasy feeling at the whole scene. A couple of his teammates wandered by, both with beautiful women hanging off their arms. One of them winked at him and jerked his chin toward the woman next to him who'd somehow managed to figure out she wasn't his type.

Parker sighed. He didn't even know his type anymore. His conscious brain rejected what this place represented, what might happen tonight. He wouldn't allow it, no matter how badly he wanted it right now.

He looked over and took in the pleasant landscape of the woman next to him, but he kept glancing back over to Nicco—the man, the legend, his rival on the field, and the one man in the room Parker should avoid, but couldn't. He watched as the guy's hands roaming all over the woman in front of him as the one behind him moved around to clutch his neck, pull him in for a long kiss as their bodies swayed, bumped, ground.

The other woman pulled her companion from Nicco's lips then landed a kiss on her mouth. Parker sucked in a breath, watching as the women fondled each other on the dance floor.

Nicco looked up and caught Parker's eye, then leaned back into the dark brown arms of Terry, who'd come up from behind and gripped his hips. Parker gulped, unable to tear his eyes away, acutely aware of the strange voyeuristic connection he'd formed with Nicco.

One of the women moved in front of Nicco again and ran her tongue down his jaw as they moved to the music. The man gripped her long black hair and pulled her close, his hand disappearing up her dress. The crowd ebbed and flowed, giving Parker enough glimpses of the couple for him to be certain what Nicco's fingers were doing.

Terry ran his hands down Nicco's arms, to his hips, miming thrusts as Nicco tended to the woman who had just shot off into the orgasmic stratosphere. As he raised his lips from hers, pulled his fingers from under her skirt and put them in his mouth, he looked right at Parker, winked, then turned the full force of his attention to Terry.

The two mean disappeared, leaving Parker to wipe the sheen of sweat from his forehead. Could a human explode from lust? If he kept watching he'd be certain to find out. Dropping into a chair in a dark corner, he gasped in surprise to find a different woman suddenly draped over him, bare arms around his neck, lips against his ear. He smiled, unwilling to be a jerk about it but equally unwilling to have her wriggling around on his already uncomfortable lap.

"Uh, yeah, hi. Um. Sorry but, you, mmfff—"

The woman's lips covered his and the hands he'd placed on her waist to lift her off him slid upward. She tasted of wine, perfume, and a salty, unfamiliar essence he couldn't place. He broke away, embarrassed at his primal reaction.

"Jesus, sorry, I'm, oh shit.

She shifted, straddled him pressing her breasts into his chest. "It's okay, sweetie." Her breath tickled his ear.

Parker leaned away at the realization that she was the one he'd been watching on the dance floor with Nicco earlier. The woman grinned at him. "You have the most amazing eyes," she whispered. He gripped her hips, held her still. The urge to fuck had never been so intense. The simple, vanilla relationship he'd shared with Christie hadn't prepared him for this. An incredible pulse of raw lust the likes of which he had never experienced made him want to shove the woman against a wall and plow into her like a rutting bull.

She licked his lips, sharing the odd taste again—salty, and somehow rich with possibility. He slid his fingers into her hair, needing something he couldn't identify, but that was causing stars to appear around the edges of his vision.

He groaned when she slipped a hand between them and lowered his zipper with little effort. "No, I'm... Holy hell." The soft velvety skin of her palm, warm and pleasant, made him suppress a groan. He sat up and leaned into her ear. "I need to fuck you. Now."

She giggled and pushed him back. "No, you don't, you adorable thing, you. Alas, I'm merely the fluffer." He stared at her, breathless, as she kept her hand busy right here in public in a clichéd dark corner of a huge nightclub in Detroit. With an effort, he slid her off him and zipped his trousers.

When he stood, she wrapped herself around him, shoved her tongue into his mouth once more before breaking away and touching the tip of his nose with her finger. "You like how I taste, don't you handsome?" He nodded, suddenly incapable of speech, his brain buzzing with lust, anger, and frustration. "I sucked Nicco's cock earlier. He came all down my throat. That's him you're tasting." She licked his lips then stepped away, pulling her tiny excuse for a skirt straight. "I think I might take you up on your offer. You are way too cute to sacrifice to him." Stunned, struck dumb with horniness, he let her take his hand and pull him up a circular set of stairs, crowded with people in various stages of make-out.

The thumping music and flashing lights made him dizzy as he followed the woman's bare legs up and up, until they stopped in a room lit with a few lamps on tables, all shrouded with gauzy curtains. He could see arms, legs, and hear noises his brain refused to register. Cocktail waitresses moved about wearing little or nothing.

His nerves rubbed raw from over stimulation, he saw his companion pull a curtain aside to reveal Nicco, Terry, and the other woman from the dance floor, sitting with a bottle of scotch and languid expressions.

"There he is." The dark skinned man draped an arm around Nicco's shoulders as he spoke. Parker sensed the dead giveaway facial flush and ducked in next to the tall Spaniard, tugging the woman with him. She giggled and put a brazen hand over his still rigid zipper, making him flinch. Terry burst out laughing. He glared around the table and picked up a glass, downing it in one fiery, agonizing gulp.

"Cut the crap, Terrance." Nicco shoved the other man off him and over onto the other woman who shrieked and let him grab her tits. Parker flushed even hotter as Nicco's voice cut through the chest-thumping music. "*Jesu*, you are so...."

"Amazing? Incredibly well hung? Talented with your cock?" Terry leaned into the woman, smiling, his dark eyes sharp and definitely angry, his voice low and rumbling.

"Shut up," Nicco said in a low, almost non-committal tone.

Parker bit back the most compelling urge he'd ever felt. The blazing in his gut burned all the way up to the back of his eyeballs. He gripped his knees under the small table and used everything he had not to put a hand to Nicco's face, to cup his rough cheek, soothe, caress, ease the tension that rolled off the older man like smoke. He sighed and sat back, letting the woman he'd been ready to fuck a few minutes ago nibble his neck and keep stroking him.

"This is surreal." He held out his glass. Might as well be drunk on top of it.

Nicco poured him a healthy splash and shot him a grin that didn't reach his eyes. "*Si*. Well, you are in one of the most surreal cities on the planet, I'd say. *Salud.*" He held up his glass and clinked it to Parker's, the irony taking his face again, replacing the moment of soft introspection.

Parker put both arms on the back of the booth and leaned his head back against the booth. The woman's lips traveled around his neck. Fingers unbuttoned his shirt, unzipped his jeans. He sighed and went into a familiar space in his head. The space where he fondled amazing soft curves, appreciated and enjoyed female bodies. Even as he always had to imagine something else, something harder, more angular and rough every time to find his release. He shifted his hips, let the alcohol buzz and his own deep need motivate him beyond his usual reticence for public displays of affection, much less public displays of utter eroticism.

"Good Christ," he gasped when lips replaced the hand. A tongue flicked and teased. Music pounded in his ears. His hands clenched into fists. The woman's soft, eager mouth was all he knew at the moment. He grunted. His hips bucked. A finger moved lower, massaging, teasing, pressing deep, making him groan.

When he opened his eyes, the woman stared at him, before covering his lips with hers, and he let her, suddenly realizing whose mouth was on him, whose throat he fucked, whose hair he fisted. He broke away as Nicco's fingertip triggered a gut-deep, earth shattering, terrifying orgasm roaring up from the soles of his feet, lighting his spinal column and exploding behind his eyes. He cried out, no longer caring if the music covered him up, thrust deep into the other man's mouth and let it happen.

Holy shit. Holy mother of....

Parker jerked away, panting, fear, terror and lust roiling in his brain, making him breathless and pissed beyond words. "Shit." He yanked his jeans up, shoved the woman out and fell to his knees in his haste to escape. What the hell had just happened? What had he done? He had to play soccer with this man. He was supposed to beat him at his own goddamned position in two days. They were...teammates.

His eyes burned. Nicco licked his lips as he stared at Parker, his dark eyes blank.

Well you did it didn't you Doc? Yes. You did. Now you are that guy. The guy you didn't want to be.

He grabbed the half empty, three-hundred-dollar bottle of Scotch and stalked away, drinking from the neck of the thing. As he made his way through the crowd, gorgeous men and women draped around him, kissing his exposed skin until he figured out he should button his shirt. But first...He smiled down at a blonde woman with the biggest, fakest tits he'd ever seen and tugged her close.

The urge to jump off the top of this building felt way too viable at the moment. He had do something to dispel the horror of the last few minutes—when he'd just gotten a fucking blowjob from Nicco Garza.

This is not me, his brain insisted as he tugged the strange girl into an alcove, shoved her up against the wall, lifted her skirt and stroked her soft, familiar folds, slipping two fingers into her, making her squirm and sigh. As he leaned over and sucked a nipple between his lips, her body shuddered in a familiar way. He groaned when she palmed his rapidly hardening cock then shoved her off him, took a slug from the bottle he'd never dropped while fingering the nameless, eager chick. She wrapped her arms around his neck.

"You're on the Black Jacks, no?" she purred, making Parker wince at his callous thoughts of *"get the fuck away from me".*

"Yeah, that's me. Soccer star." He grimaced at her and stomped away, knocking back the burning brown liquor, trying to find the steps so he could escape this utter nightmare. He stumbled, the floor having become suddenly unreliable under his feet. A strong hand gripped his biceps. He looked at it then up at its owner's face.

"Don't touch me," he growled, jerking his arm out of Nicco's grasp.

"I am not that guy, okay. I don't, I can't, shit!" He lifted the bottle to his mouth, but the other man took it.

"Go easy, *amigo*," he crooned. Parker squinted, tried to get the two Niccos to form into one, then gave up and sank into a chair, head in his hands. The room resumed its nauseating spin. He sensed the other man's face near his, but he shifted away unwilling to be near him lest he give in to what he truly wanted. Because it simply could not happen. They were pro athletes, and he would be damned if he disappointed his parents one more time by being gay.

A tall glass of ice water appeared, and he drained it, willing the other man away from him. Didn't work. The tall, dark figure pulled a chair up alongside him and draped an arm over his shoulders. Parker braced himself for sarcasm, for innuendo, for the usual bullshit spewing from the guy's lips.

"I'm sorry." His soft Spanish lilt made Parker clench his eyes shut. *"Querido. Lo siento.* I should not have done that to you." The man put a hand on his thigh, kept his lips near Parker's ear.

"It's fine."

"No, you silly polite American, it's not. I took terrible advantage of you." The hand stroked, soothed, the musical voice calmed Parker's pounding heart. "Be pissed off. You have every right. But...." Nicco turned his chin with a light touch. "You are..." He dropped his gaze, surprising Parker. "Amazing."

He pressed his full lips to Parker's once, in a chaste, dissatisfying way, then stood. Parker watched as the one Nicco morphed into two again, heard the two of them speak. "Get water and some sleep, young Parker. We have a big day ahead on Monday." He tilted Parker's face up to his, ran a rough thumb over his lips making Parker's entire body shiver. Then he walked away without another word, hands in his pockets.

Parker watched him go, his heart sinking. What had he done? How in God's name could he play now with the man whose dark eyes and full lips made him want to weep with desire? He lurched to his feet, stumbled down the circular staircase and out into the cool night air.

Chapter Ten

R afe stirred and rolled over, reaching out for Maureen's soft familiar curves. When he hit the living room floor fully awake, he was staring at the rug, and instantly recalled the verbal knock-down, drag-out that had landed him on the too-short couch. Adam dropped into a nearby chair, holding a bowl of cereal.

"Hey, uh, Mom's in the bathroom alternating cursing and crying. I figured you should know."

Rafe groaned and got to his feet. He had been pushing the team to its collective limit through two months of camp in between managing bouts of seriously bad behavior on the part of various players. The daily stress of setting plays, getting a group of extreme sports egos to actually work together, keeping as much of the bullshit out of the media as possible while placating a set of needy investors had proven overwhelming. The added bonus of his prized coach delaying his appearance until a week before their first game only added to the frustration.

So when Maureen had some kind of breakdown last night after a dinner party at Jack and Sara's house to celebrate the eve of their first game, he'd snapped. Too much booze at dinner, too many veiled innuendoes about team dynamics not working and general behavioral problems and too much denial about his role as the husband of a pregnant woman played hell with his nerves. He had no real excuse.

He'd made muttered apologies, leaving Sara glaring at her husband, and they'd left. The tense car ride home ended with tears from his wife and more fury from him.

He knocked on the bathroom door. "Honey? You okay?"

"Go away." She sniffled. "Far, far away. Go back to the team. Sleep there. I'll see you at the end of the season."

"C'mon, babe. I'm really sorry. I was an ass."

"Yeah."

"I know I was." Adam tapped his shoulder, held out a steaming cup of something that smelled like lilacs. Rafe smiled. "Adam brought your favorite tea."

"Go the fuck away, Rafe, I mean it. Sorry, Adam."

The tall kid shrugged and patted Rafe's arm. "No worries. She'll be okay. Let's eat. You've got a big day."

Rafe put his aching head against the door, ignoring his stepson's attempt at adulthood. "Please, Maureen. I am really sorry. I need you today."

"Yeah, should have thought of that before you called me—what was it? Oh yes...."

"Maureen, come on. I didn't call you anything. You were making too much noise for me to even get a word in." He stopped, realizing that was the wrong road to head down. "Listen, I've been behaving badly. I haven't been here for you. It's partly your fault, you know. You're so goddamned independent, you've set me up. I don't even know what I do for you. How you even need me."

The door jerked open. He met his wife's beautiful, watery blue eyes. His chest tightened again. Dear God, he was so stupid. These fucking boys parading as men he'd been babysitting, threatening, coddling into working for him and not against him—they did not matter. This, right in front of him, mattered above all else. He took her hand, pulled her close, covered her face with kisses, and muttered any and everything he could think of to make her stop crying.

"Stop it." She pushed him away and brushed at her eyes. "Rafe, we're a partnership. That implies need. What you don't have, I give you. What I can't do, you can. Don't you get it? You brought this into my life, gave me a reason to trust you, to believe you're here for me. You've essentially disappeared. I get why but I don't like it. Not now. Not with all this." She put a hand on the shelf of her belly.

He reached out for her, heart on fire with anguish, head buzzing with terror at the sight of her pale skin, the dark circles under her eyes. She leaned on the wall, hands to the small of her back. He ran his hands across her shoulders, down her arms, leaned in to kiss her amazing lips. She ducked out his embrace and made her slow way down the hall, calling for Adam to heat the tea back up.

Rafe watched her go, helpless frustration at his current predicament building in his chest. He pulled his seemingly forever buzzing phone out of his shorts pocket, grimacing at the sight of his assistant's number.

Choosing to ignore it, he followed Mo into the kitchen and glued a smile on his face, determined to fix this. She turned her face up to his when he leaned over her, hand on her huge stomach. Then blew out a breath and shoved him away.

"God, my back is killing me." She let him kiss her, put her hand against his cheek, making the band around his chest release slightly. He crouched next to her.

"Aren't we, I mean, isn't this…" He stared at her stomach, anxiety strangling him. She put a hand on his hair.

"Yeah, honey. Today is your baby's due date. And the first day of your season. Perfect timing once again."

He groaned and leaned into her, putting his lips against the taut skin of her belly, whispering, "Wait, young Inez. Hang on, my man. Give me twenty-four hours, *por favor*?"

Rafe glanced up at Maureen, fear sending a fresh thrill of stress down his spine. She looked like her whole body hurt. He really should have read some of those "what to expect" books. He'd only made it to one damn breathing class or whatever they called it. He closed his eyes. Sweet Jesus, help him, he could not do this.

His phone buzzed again. "Sorry, it's Jack." He stood.

She waved him away and kept staring out the window. He frowned and sat and took the call.

"Dude, please tell me you did not piss off my sister any more than you did my own lovely bride last night."

"Can we talk about the team instead please?"

"Sorry. As Sara has in no uncertain terms informed me for the last, oh, ten hours straight—you have a priorities problem. And I am your enabler, or some shit."

"She's right." Rafe stood, walked around behind Maureen and rubbed her shoulders, keeping the phone propped against his shoulder. "But we've informed the young Master Inez he should save his appearance for another day or so." Maureen leaned her head on his hand.

"I'm coming with you," she stated loud enough for her brother to hear it through the phone.

"Oh hell, no," Jack sputtered into his ear. "She'll distract you and, ow! Shit, Sara, cut it out."

"We'll figure it out, don't worry. I'm gonna go. Go control your woman already." He ended the call, dropped the phone on the table, and leaned down to kiss his wife's lips.

"Do what you want, Maureen. I know I can't stop you. But if you guys are coming with me, you gotta get it together. I need to be there in about two hours. *Vamanos!*" He headed down the hall to the shower, hoping his leapfrogging nerves would calm, but realizing the day had only just begun.

* * * *

PARKER WENT THROUGH his usual pre-game ritual—running five miles and consuming a four egg omelet with a cup of coffee and orange juice. The past months had been a blur of sheer physical stress and strain and avoidance of anything resembling up close and personal time with one Nicolas Garza. They'd battled it out, giving each other mutual black eyes more than once during fifty-fifty battles for the ball, and Parker had loved the contact—had relished the minutes he got to spend so close to a perfect example of a classic midfielder.

He'd remained strictly professional, never lingering long in the locker room and keeping to himself or with the more low-key members of the team, such as Kago and the Germans. He'd even been approached by an agent and had entered into discussions about representation.

"You'll need a place to land once this little experiment goes pear-shaped, Parker," the guy had insisted. "And you are the real deal. Not like all these has-beens."

Parker had been named captain and as the attacking mid with Nicco on his left wing. Many claimed Nicco had caused such external strife for the team in general, getting photographed in any number of compromising positions, he'd put the whole experiment in jeopardy already. But Parker didn't care. He was determined that the team would succeed.

This pre-season start-up was absolutely crucial. He'd been over to Rafe's house for dinner, met his amazingly cool and very pregnant wife and her son from an earlier marriage. They discussed tactics, concepts, personalities and the competition for hours. And for the first time he felt truly needed, a part of something important.

He glanced down at his phone, noting the name he'd programmed in a few weeks ago. Sighing, he answered, acknowledging the surge of undeniable ambivalence. "Hey, Ashley."

"Just wanted to wish you good luck," his girlfriend said. "Miss you."

He ran a hand down his face. Ashley Klein had fallen into his lap more or less, at a team bonding event. She worked in the marketing department and happened to be a dead ringer for Christie. When he'd spotted her across the room blatantly staring at him, he'd lifted his juice glass at her pretty smile. By the end of the night he had her back in a dark corner, kissing her with something approaching desperation.

The next morning he'd actually been shocked to find her in his bed, snuggled down into his chest. So, now, apparently, he had an official girlfriend. Who, thankfully, proved the opposite of Christie personality-wise. Undemanding, busy with her own job, not clingy or needy, but a damn tiger between the sheets. Ashley could be what any man hoped for in a girlfriend. Parker hated himself for staying so disconnected from her, using her body to take his edge off, to quell the near constant level of lust he lived with daily. She, however, didn't seem to mind or resent it. She left him alone when he needed and appeared when he wanted.

"Thanks. We'll be fine, I think. I hope. I don't know." The butterflies beating the inside of his stomach transformed into small bats making him a little nauseated. "See you after?" he asked weakly, not even caring, but knowing he was supposed to ask.

"Maybe," she said breezily, making him grateful in a way that sickened him. He needed her but he knew why—she kept him from facing himself, from acknowledging he would play this season and then get his shiny new agent to find him something else.

He could not play with Nicco. No matter they formed the middle of a strong team. Their chemistry on the pitch was undeniable. The press that had been allowed to watch some early scrimmages commented on it—how the two of them seemed to be able to anticipate each other's moves before they made them. Which would be key to winning in a new league surprisingly stacked with talented players.

"Parker," she said, sounding a million miles away.

He blinked, realized he'd been drifting, pondering exactly how much he enjoyed playing the game he loved with Nicolas Garza. "Sorry, babe. What?"

"Nothing...." Her voice faded. "Just...play well. I'll be watching."

"Okay. Thanks." He hung up. Dropping the phone to the floor of his rented loft overlooking the Detroit River, he allowed himself a few minutes of remorse. She deserved better. He resolved to break it off with her after this game. He was obviously incapable of real emotion, so embroiled he was in his own mind with Nicco.

The thought of coming back to an empty condo after the game today made him twitchy. He toyed with calling her back, asking her to meet him afterward, for dinner, for anything. But he let it go.

The intervening weeks had been tough beyond imagining as the Detroit summer edged away and the temperatures eased down into the seventies. The lack of humidity provided a nice break to his Southern-bred thin blood. The covered, state-of-the-art venue had inevitable delays but had its grand opening. The team got exactly one full workout on its artificial turf after the giant, ribbon-cutting opening ceremony.

Tempers ran short and hot among the team and its coaches. Frustrated by delays and the onslaught of media plus all their extra chores online, the men still put in near nightly appearances at high-visibility fundraisers and other boring events. After all the drama, the stress, and brutal practices in the summer sun, the day had arrived—their first official game as a team.

Rafe scheduled aggressively, putting together a nice mix of gimmie games and challenging matches. The new coach, once he'd finally shown, had proved as tough as everyone had warned. The tall, dark Turk with the terrible tragedy lurking in his past seemed to embrace the conflict roiling through the players' ranks. He even egged on some of the more volatile players, coaxing higher levels of play with his harsh but apparently effective words. Willing them to explode with fury for the express purpose of showing them how immature they had acted.

Parker emerged from the shower, rubbing his hair, ignoring his body's clamor for more physical contact. His phone buzzed again—Nicco.

Parker's scalp tingled, and he contemplated ignoring the call. But the two men had formed a bond around the concept of a winning season—they were both fierce competitors. Plus, for all his bullshit, all the drama seeming to trail after him like fog, Garza was a stone-cold pro at the game. He had a fiercely strategic mind when it came to breaking down opponents since he'd played against many members of opposing teams in Europe.

He and Parker had spent several hours evaluating the team's strengths and weaknesses with both Rafe and the new coach. He blew out a breath and answered the call.

. . . .

NICCO SAT, NURSING a giant pitcher of ice water and fist full of painkillers, gazing out the window of his newly-rented condo in Royal Oak. He knew damn good and well avoiding temptation by placing himself a solid forty-minute ride away from downtown had been wise in theory. While his natural inclination for constant input, for physical and mental stimulation, kept him dipping into pools of debauchery. Much to the chagrin of his new coaches and the club's constantly yammering public relations and social media minions.

He'd ditched Terrance and taken up with a girl he'd met at a club about a month ago. She provided the sort of caretaking that soothed him, staying over and making breakfast, coffee, doing his laundry. She never asked for much in return, which made Nicco face and embrace his total shithead most days. He was honestly satisfied with both men and women sexually speaking. But something drove him to a female after Terry—if for no other reason than to dispel the near constant low-lying level of horny he sustained over his teammate, Parker Rollings.

Playing with the guy hadn't helped. They'd clicked as if they shared a brain on the field, which shocked him. He'd always been a lone ranger, the superstar buoyed by a supporting cast of normal men. Parker proved soccer truly is a beautiful game— he was a dancer in motion, an amazing blur of arms, legs, torso, his footwork nothing less than exquisite. Shocked he was playing at this expansion level, and he hadn't ended up at least in the major league soccer ranks if not in one of the premiere European leagues, Nicco's desire to have him grew stronger along with his respect.

He sighed, and clutched his phone, an unfamiliar nervousness taking hold. Before he knew it, he'd pulled up a number, stared at it a minute then put the device to his ear.

"*Hola.*"

"Yeah, what's up?" Parker answered, his voice the usual blend of polite interest and deflection.

Nicco put a hand over his eyes. Why had he called the guy? Parker epitomized the phrase "cool as a cucumber," keeping his wits at his crucial position, a natural leader on the field. Poor kid took no end of shit from the rest of the team for his tendency to blush bright red at any provocation. Nicco adored watching him, playing against him and being in his general vicinity, so much that he'd caught himself fantasizing about him with alarming regularity.

Didn't help he'd manipulated the poor kid into a position so he, Nicco, knew exactly what to expect down under as it were—and he had never forgotten it. He wanted more but remained convinced Parker couldn't handle it. Besides, he'd seen the new girlfriend hanging off his arm. They made a lovely couple.

"Watch out for Bolo today." He named the striker for Orlando, the established team they faced in their inaugural game. "He's got a wicked bad habit of high cleats when he gets frustrated. You will frustrate him I am certain."

"Oh, yeah, thanks."

Silence swirled between them. Parker spoke, making Nicco's pulse race. "You're pretty amazing, you know. Don't think I've said that yet."

Nicco snorted, tried to get the image of Parker in his arms as far out of his head as possible. "No, I'm just a plodder. I practice a lot. I'm over the hill, as I'm reminded daily watching all you youngsters."

"Spare me, Nicco. False modesty doesn't suit you."

He laughed. "Nailed, as it were." He sank into his seat, ran a hand down his face. "Okay, I'm good. I know it. But you, young Parker, you are...."

"Spare *me*, will you?"

"Fine. Watch Bolo. See you in a few hours." He stood and stretched, hoping a shower would chill his ramped-up libido at the sound of the other man's warm, American southern accent.

"Nicco?"

He stopped, gripped the phone so hard his hand ached. "Hmm?" Attempts to sound casual when nearly dying of lust proved harder than he'd thought.

"Thanks."

Trying not to beg to let him prove how great they could be together, Nicco ground out, "For what?"

"For showing me how to play the game at this level. Proving to me I can do it. You pushed me harder than anyone, and I know it."

"Oh, uh, sure. Well, you know, I'm a natural born teacher."

Parker's easy laughter made him smile. "Well, natural born something, but anyways, thanks. See you in a few."

Nicco stared at the phone, willing the man back to his ear, then finally set it on the table and flopped down on the bed. He couldn't play like this—pent up, horny, moony over some kid who barely even realized what he wanted out of life. Didn't take long to get it done, as images floated through his head of Parker, of his strong torso, and deep blue eyes.

Chapter Eleven

Rafe paced the office as Maureen propped her feet up on a chair and flipped through the glossy, full-color program and Adam studied the team's classroom white board. He replayed the scenes over and over again. The potentially disastrous set-pieces that had gone off without a hitch, the hat trick his amazing young midfielder had managed, a last-minute substitution when his star German defensive back went down on a yellow card foul for the asshole Bolo. And finally the breathtaking final goal by the team's number one troublemaker, bringing him to the score at the end.

Detroit 4. Orlando 3.

Their first game, an exhibition against a legitimate soccer team, in the rearview mirror finally—with a victory to boot.

Holy shit. He felt the goofy grin encompass his entire face once again, heard the loud yelling and celebration in the locker room next door.

"Go already, Jesus," Maureen smiled at him from across the room. "Celebrate with them." She made her slow way over to him and put her arms around his neck. "I'm fine. We're fine."

He leaned down and kissed his wife, long and deep. She put a hand to his face. Adam cleared his throat, loudly.

"Cut it out guys. Can I go with you to the locker room? Please?" Maureen shot him a look of disapproval.

He was about to agree when Jack and Sara burst into the room. Jack held a half empty bottle of expensive champagne and handed it to him.

"Drink up, *mi hermano.* Here's to the ballsiest game of soccer I have ever seen. Well the fuck done." He smacked Rafe on the shoulder and grinned like an idiot.

"You boys carry on." Maureen put a hand to her back, bringing Rafe right down to the Earth where he was scheduled to become a father at any moment. "Sara, can you run me home?"

"Maybe." His sister-in-law shot him one of her patented about-to-administer-a-lecture looks.

"Hang on a sec." Rafe put the champagne bottle on his desk and stopped Maureen before she left. "Honey, I need to be with you. I mean...." He touched her stomach, waited for the usual shifting under his palm. It didn't come. He frowned and moved his hand lower. She batted him away.

"I'm fine. Go. Be with the team. Then get your ass home. You owe me a foot rub. This kid of yours is about to beat me to death from the inside." She pressed her lips to his, making his heart beat faster, like it always did when he realized his luck. "I'm proud of you, Rafe. Well the fuck done indeed."

He watched, speechless as she let her brother kiss her cheek and rub her stomach, then waddled out.

"You sure know how to time things, my man." Jack grabbed the champagne and started out the door. "Now let's go see the room full of men-boys who are gonna get us the first expansion league championship."

Rafe shook his head and followed the other man down the hall.

• • • •

A ROAR OF PLEASURE made Nicco turn from his locker and smile as the young assistant coach entered the room trailed by a suit, one of the team's funding sources or something. Metin, the surly Turkish coach had already slapped everyone on the back and left, muttering about getting home.

Nicco had come as close to feeling warm and fuzzy as a guy like him got, watching Sevim's progress in the past few weeks. He had known the man well—they'd been teammates for a time on the Madrid team. What had happened to him should never happen to any man. If the rumors were true and he now had his shit together on all fronts, Nicco wished him nothing but the best.

He shook his head, recalling the match. It had been a fucking gutsy playbook. Long on tricks, passing, and heavy-handed defense and less about attacking than he liked, but the men had executed it to perfection, throwing off Orlando's run-and-gun style. This damn thing might work, he mused, watching as the team patted Rafe's back and passed around beers and champagne.

"Well done, ya raging bastard." Rafe stopped in front of Nicco, arms crossed. "Please confirm for me that your celebration plans do not include farm animals or hookers. The PR department can't take the stress."

Nicco shrugged. "No promises, *paesono*. Must keep my options open." His eyes betrayed him, strayed to the left and caught Parker facing his locker, the taut muscles of his currently bare ass begging for Nicco's caress. Rafe's hand on his arm brought him back from fantasy land. He smirked, hoping to deflect. "Why? You inviting me over for farm games?"

"Don't," the young coach whispered.

"What?" Nicco pulled his arm out of the man's grip. But he knew damn well what.

"Leave him alone. I mean it, Garza."

"Fuck off, Coach, with all due respect. I know what I'm—"

Rafe cut him off. "He's a good kid. Don't ruin him."

Nicco rolled his eyes but his gut burned. He knew he had to stop all the fantasizing before it went any further. Parker had a full life ahead of him. An amazing young talent, who'd doubtless soon have the soccer world at his feet—what could Nicco offer him? Nothing but a washed-up, dirty old man history. Nothing good would come of a connection, as much as his body ached for it. Corrupting the innocent best stay off his to-do list. Now that his coach had spelled it out for him Nicco embraced the reality.

"Okay." He settled his face into neutral lines. "Relax. Jesus."

Rafe let go of his arm and walked over to his team captain, the man in question, who'd donned dark jeans and a stark white button down shirt. Nicco watched, trying like hell to suppress the surging need to touch, to kiss, to possess, but the three-foot chasm between them remained too wide.

• • • •

PARKER'S HEAD SPUN and his heart still pounded with residual adrenaline. He jumped at the sensation of Rafe's arm around his shoulders.

"Amazing work, Rollings. Truly. Thank you."

Parker smiled, let himself relax, but he couldn't shake the tingly sensation all over his skin. His eyes met the dark ones over Rafe's shoulder then darted away.

"Sure, yeah, I mean it was pretty awesome." Rafe grinned at him, pulled his phone from his pocket, and frowned at the screen. Parker grabbed his arm, alarmed at the way the man's face drained of color. "Nicco!" he barked out, trying to get someone's attention.

Nicco appeared on Rafe's other side and they eased Rafe down onto the bench.

"What's wrong?" The coach's phone slipped from his hand and bounced across the floor. Jack picked up and looked at it.

"Oh hell...."

"What?" Parker demanded. "Where's Fred?" he glanced around for their trainer, a retired physician. Jack pulled Rafe to his feet.

Fred took one look at the coach's pale face and smiled. Jack stared around, at a loss it seemed, a rare occurrence for him. "Let's go," the tall white-haired gentlemen said. "Move out of the way, you assholes. It's time for the real work to begin."

Rafe walked out without a word, dazed-looking, flanked by the other two men. The team hooted and clapped, patted his shoulder as he passed them.

"Damn, I thought he was gonna pass out for a minute there." Parker sat, sensed Nicco next to him and had to shut his eyes against the urge to lean into him, to clutch his face, to feel something, anything, as long as it was the other man's flesh under his fingers.

He stood, grabbed the keys to his new car, his new condo, and started out, needing space to process the events of the last three hours.

"Parker! Don't forget, we've got that party...." Kago called after him. But Parker ignored him, making a mental note to text an apology. He needed to be alone.

Chapter Twelve

Six Months Later

S Parker stared at the screen, unwilling to process the information glowing, like an omen on his web browser. "It's official. A Black Jack Gentlemen comes out as the first openly gay soccer player."

He stood up, his chest pounding. After pacing around the room for a few minutes he sat back down, still unwilling to acknowledge Nicco had done it. He'd insinuated it to Parker at their last practice, telling him he'd made a decision about something and he hoped it didn't screw up the team's dynamic. But he was through pretending.

He'd pinned Parker with such a gaze at that moment, as they stood facing each other across a fifty-fifty ball during a squad scrimmage, Parker had a tough time shaking it off and moving his legs. He'd known then what it had to be. So now, there it sat in black and white on his screen. He could practically hear the sports universe convulsing in response.

"Goddamn it," he muttered, trying to parse why he had an urge to call the man, to talk to him, ask him why he'd done such a crazy thing. Parker had deepened his reliance on Ashley, on her calm, reassuring presence in his life. Her ability to organize a party, or an outing, or just about anything astonished him daily. It reminded him of his mother, really, if he were honest with himself. But he still fantasized nearly non-stop about his dark, compelling teammate.

Ashley never demanded anything more of him than what he wanted to give. They had sex on a regular basis, usually at his place, in his darkened bedroom. Its quiet predictability was a relief in a way, familiar and reassuring—but mechanical, not much more than simple physical release.

Nicolas, on the other hand, had been embroiled in a public and very dramatic relationship with a wealthy, semi-divorced socialite. The sex party rumors about her giant mansion in the suburbs rampantly smeared over every possible soccer tabloid, making the most splash overseas, where soccer players enjoyed celebrity status. The woman loved nothing more than making loud declarations of her abiding love for "her Nicco".

For his part, Nicco always smiled for the cameras, forever accompanying her to glitzy events, walking red carpets wearing tuxedos, looking as amazing as ever.

They had maintained their closeness on the field, combining leadership styles to guide the Black Jacks to a winning season. The whole thing had been a blur to Parker. He could hardly wait to get to practice every day, to see Nicco, to talk to him, to feel the other man's body against his during scrimmages.

They laughed, joked, slapped ass with the rest of the team for a few hours every day—a few hours that kept Parker going until the next day. More and more he would close his eyes as he entered Ashley's welcoming body and dream of Nicco under his hands, of the man's hips, and ass grinding against his. The entire concept of having sex with a man intimidated Parker, but he knew as well as he knew his own shoe size, he wanted it with Nicolas Garza, badly. Even if just for one time, to break the tension and prove, perhaps, his fevered imagination had transformed the whole thing into something more than a physical act.

The season had ended, as they all do. The Black Jacks emerged as champions of the expansion soccer league's regular season. Parker had pulled a hamstring in the final game, which went well with his broken thumb thanks to a clumsy fall he'd made, and a suspected foot stress fracture. He had more money in the bank than he could spend, a willing girlfriend in his bed, and a brutal crush on a fellow teammate.

A teammate who had decided to become the poster boy for gay pro athletes while at the same time dumping his famous and very wealthy socialite girlfriend. Gutsy, Parker would concede. Twitter had erupted with support and vitriol, but Parker decided to ignore it.

He had a meeting with his agent this afternoon to ask for a transfer. As much as he truly loved this team and what he'd done for it, he had to get the hell away from Nicco. The concept of being "the gay soccer player's boyfriend" was just too much for him to take. Besides, considering Nicco his "boyfriend" involved more jumping of the gun than Parker wanted to contemplate.

Since the lone, bizarre encounter at the club where Nicco had blown him, while tricking him to thinking a girl did it, he had been all business. Behaving in an utterly professional, jovial, just-buddies, manner without a hint of anything more, which killed Parker daily.

He saw an email drop into his inbox from Jack, stating the board's full support of Nicolas Garza's recent revelation, hoping Nicco's teammates would not consider this to have any effect on the man's playing ability or his crucial contribution to the Black Jacks' success. The hard fact remained—Nicco had been key to the team's winning season. He'd thrown himself into the effort with every ounce of his considerable energy, rallying players who flagged, propping up others who slumped, berating those who slacked. Acting in a way that surprised former coaches and teammates alike—as if he wanted to be part of a team and not the lone superstar.

Now, he'd ruined everything and forced Parker's hand. He had to go. If Nicco were out he had no more excuses. If the pro soccer world was ready for a gay player, then it could be ready for a couple in an openly gay relationship. While Parker wanted nothing more in the world than to play hard, practice harder, then go home with Nicco he knew it wouldn't work.

He loved to hear the man laugh—a harsh-sounding thing at first until he'd gotten used to it. The guy's propensity for practical jokes found many targets, which had finally made him accepted by his fellow players, especially once he'd proven himself so adept at leading them to victories.

Parker adored the sing-songy cadence of his voice, the way he was so single-minded about the game. Their weekly strategy sessions impressed Parker even more. Nicco could be a coach, someday.

He frowned, bit his lip, and recalled an odd conversation and near close encounter they'd had one night toward the end of the season after the rest of the team had showered and left. Leaving the two of them, battered and bruised, mainly from going head to head against each other.

Parker had looked up to find the locker room echoing and empty and Nicco sitting a few feet away. The look in the man's eyes had been sad, remorseful, with a finality that startled Parker. "What's up?" he asked, keeping it casual as he got to his feet. He groaned and stretched out his newly sore elbow and tried to work out a kink in his back. He'd missed the trainer's attention and would need a double treatment tomorrow just to suit up and play.

"I was married once, you know," the handsome Spaniard had stated apropos of nothing.

Parker had winced as he lifted his practice jersey off and touched his sore ribs. "Well, I hope you didn't beat on her like you just did on me," he said, mildly, not realizing how suggestive it sounded until it had escaped his lips. He felt the familiar flush creep up his neck to his face.

A warm smile had spread over Nicco's sweaty face. "No." He stood, turned to his own locker, and started to undress.

"I heard about her." Parker had been unable to rip his eyes from the sight of Nicco's lean, strong back. "Saw some pictures. I followed the Euro league pretty closely once upon a time." He gave up on standing when Nicco stepped out of his shorts and stood still facing away from Parker. He had intimate knowledge of the subtle strength of the man's body—he boasted the sore ribs, black eyes, and scuffed skin to prove it. His mouth dried out as his gaze stayed glued to Nicco's backside.

"Yeah, I guess you did, being the youngster you are." Nicco's voice had been soft. He'd wandered over to the towel shelf, grabbed one, and fastened it around his waist before crossing his arms and spearing him with a glacial stare.

"Don't call me youngster," he'd squeaked out, wincing at the sound of his voice. "She left you, spilled the beans about you...your...."

"Boyfriend," Nicco's voice had been strong, firm, in command of the situation. Parker felt like a blithering idiot with his gaping stare and constantly blushing face as Nicco continued. "Yes. She was fun for a while. Loved to look good, spend money, show off. It was more or less required of me to obtain one—you know, a wife." He shrugged, "I never loved her." He sat, suddenly, as if deflated. He put his head in his hands.

Parker had risen as if in a trance and closed the gap between them. He'd put a hand on Nicco's bare shoulder. He was dying to soothe the man, to assure him it was okay, people made mistakes. Nicco's outer persona—cocky, confident, aware of his extreme talent on the pitch—remained at odds with the man he saw right now. Parker had always sensed a deep unhappiness, a restlessness that lent itself to sometimes bizarre, unexplainable bad choices.

Nicco kept his head down. Parker removed his hand, but gulped when the man moved fast, gripping his wrist and standing so their bare chests had mere inches between them.

"Don't," Parker had whispered, drunk with desire and wishing for nothing more than Nicco to read his body language and ignore his single word of denial. Nicco's exotic face with its huge chocolate-brown eyes, strong nose, and firm jaw loomed, as if pondering the options.

Then he stepped away, let go of Parker's wrist, confusion and unhappiness back in his expression. "I mean...." Parker's arm remained suspended in the air as though Nicco still had hold of him.

"No," Nicco had said, spinning on his heel and heading back to his locker. He yanked out street clothes, dressy, as was required of them. No jeans or sweats or slouchy appearances allowed when entering or exiting the Black Jacks' facility—they all agreed to this in their contracts. He kept muttering under his breath in Spanish while Parker stared frozen with indecision.

"Wait," he'd said, furious for sounding like such a dork but no longer caring.

"No, you wait." Nicco had rounded on him, tucking his dress shirt into his pants over his un-showered skin. "You...just wait," he growled, stepping over to Parker again, glowering, breathing heavy. "Wait for someone better, young Parker. I am no good for you. As tempting as you are." Parker flushed red again as Nicco raked his gaze up and down his near-naked and obviously aroused form. "I need to get out of here," he muttered, raising a hand as if to touch Parker's face then spitting out a curse and stomping out.

Parker sank to the bench, then rose to take his shower, put on his own dress clothes, and left in a daze wondering what he had nearly done.

Now, he sat here warring internally over a recent experiment. He'd located an exclusive, private, tropical club catering to the "man who requires discretion and has the money to afford it." A gay vacation club—because he needed to do this thing. He needed to have sex with a man and get past it. To stop building it up in his head as this perfect...thing. It was just sex, for Christ's sake. Pleasant, for a few moments, then over, a release of tension, nothing more or less.

So he had submitted an application, nervous and terrified someone would find out but relying on the "discretion guarantee," especially once he paid their jaw-dropping fee.

His scalp tingled at the sight of a new email appearing that instant confirming his reservation. He was invited to enjoy the casual, relaxed and completely private atmosphere four weeks from today.

His hands shook. He clenched them together in his lap and spent a few moments regretting ever laying eyes on Nicco Garza. This was not Nicco's fault. Parker had suspected his own homosexual leanings for years but had never acted on them. So, now he would, if five thousand dollars' worth of travel and discretion guarantees were to be believed.

His phone buzzed across the table next to the computer. He glanced at it, his face heating up at the sight of Nicco's name on the screen. How in the hell did the man always manage to call him at the wrong moment? He shoved the thing to the floor, cursing and already regretting the money spent, the move to Detroit, the breakup with Christie, and the flagrant nose-thumbing to his parents.

He should be in medical school right now, done with year one, and likely in the midst of a wedding planning month. Not sitting here contemplating how Nicco's lips felt that night, how close he had come to kissing him in the locker room, and how much he yearned for his touch.

He glared at the soccer news page again. If expansion teams qualified for playoffs, they'd been in them now. For now, their first season was over with only a few injuries and his pondering running away from the team. Nicco had come out, made a publicly gay declaration and would no doubt weather the storm with little backlash. God knew his entire career had been nothing but one long gossip column.

Parker himself had been named to an infamous "Fab 5" hottest new footie men on a notorious European soccer fan Instagram account, debuting at Number Three. Their obsession with soccer player torsos, asses, and legs embarrassed the shit out of him. He'd done the requisite interview, his face beet red the entire time, and had been dubbed "baby boy Parker" by the crew, which now stuck fast with his teammates.

His body ached from the past months of daily torture, but his heart hurt worse. He'd give anything to be playing right now, finishing off an amazing season with a run at a championship designation. The team management had been assured next year there would be such a thing. Parker relaxed and forced himself to look at the email again.

"Your travel itinerary to La Luna, our exclusive resort in the Maldives is included. As a new member, you will be paired with another newbie for the first night. If it works for you guys, great! If not, we will gladly make the necessary room changes. However, we match carefully and are very rarely proven wrong! See you soon."

He noted the flight details then went for a run, coming up with a million excuses not to go and one reason he had to. Nicolas Garza. He had to dislodge the man from his psyche. If it took an exotic week of fucking some strange guy until he couldn't walk, then so be it. He'd go, get his man love cherry popped, and be over it pure and simple.

Chapter Thirteen

N icco sat in a soft chair, fresh-squeezed orange juice in one hand, feet up on the railing, enjoying a soft ocean breeze. He tried to relax and to keep his heart from pounding out of his chest. This had been such a stupid idea. Almost as epic as the one he'd made a few weeks ago, barging into Rafe's office and declaring himself ready to be the guy, the one who came out as a pro athlete.

He'd dumped the crazy bitch with the sex parties and the coke addiction after waking up one morning in a tangle of arms and legs and God knows what else, his head pounding and his heart yearning for one thing—Parker Rollings.

That morning he had gone home, taken a shower, and stared at himself in the mirror for a solid thirty minutes before driving down to the Black Jacks complex and making his pronouncement to the assistant coach.

"Okay," Rafe had said, leaning back, his son strapped to his chest in some sort of contraption. "I'll alert the marketing department. You know you have my personal support, right?"

"Yeah," Nicco had said, nervousness running up and down his spine like rats' feet. "So what happens now?"

What happened came quickly and included a solid month of interviews up one side and down the other by every sports, news, and gossip channel. He'd gone on late night talk shows, mid-day women's shows, you name it he'd been there, declaring his extreme gayness to the world.

Of course, technically he was bi-sexual, but didn't have the energy to explain how it gave him double the opportunities. So he left that part out. A sick sort of publicity web got woven around him, thanks to his own words and actions. He got a shit ton of hate email, twitter messages, the works, but none of it bothered him. Because the one man he wanted to be out for would have nothing to do with him.

Parker and Ashley remained the happy, pretty, and perfectly hetero couple. He had no one. As the gay-boy darling of the press, the brave man who'd risked his career to declare truth to the world or however the marketing department was spinning it, he decided he deserved a vacation. To a ridiculously expensive and far away gay club where he could fuck his way through as many handsome men as he wanted.

He'd heard of La Luna but had dismissed it as excessive and unnecessary. He had all the sex he wanted, until now, of course. So he paid their extortionist fees, and here he sat. Since he was now a minor celebrity, he got priority booking it seemed.

His team had been supportive up to a point. He'd known better than to pull this stunt during the season. His shrink had called him because Nicco had skipped his last two appointments, worried about his motivation for such an announcement.

Nicco had laughed and told him he'd never felt more free, more unencumbered, albeit a little lonely. The man had sighed in his ear, made noises about "negative motivations" and "more talk therapy" so Nicco had hung up on him.

Then he'd dropped to the floor of his condo and let tears slip from his eyes, finally succumbing to real chest-heaving sobs. He cried like a woman—for Leandro, and for Parker before he fell into exhausted asleep right on the hardwood.

The fallout had been immense but mostly in a positive direction, which had shocked him. A month after the fact, Nicco stood, ensconced in the public eye as a celebrity, a hero for the gay athletes everywhere. Handsome, mature, fit, successful, rich, and homosexual, forever and ever, amen.

He sighed then startled when the door in the suite behind him rattled and swung open. His chair tipped too far back, dumping him onto the terrace floor. "Shit, mother fucker goddammit!" He scrambled up, rubbing the back of his head, and found a towel to wipe the juice off his new linen shorts. His face burned and the acid in his gut bubbled up another notch. Why in the hell he'd be nervous when he faced nothing a week of screwing, then back to life as usual, escaped him.

Of course, he did have to make a decision in between all the fucking—about whether or not to stay in the States during the offseason. More importantly if he'd exercise his option to stay with the Detroit project. His agent had been screaming at him to get out of it. A couple of major league soccer teams had been nosing around until his Big Gay Announcement. Right after, his agent would only return every other one of his calls. Until the positive media onslaught, which seemed to remind said agent of Nicco's future contribution to his agency's bank account.

Nicco had developed a soft spot for the Motor City, and the thought of never getting to see Parker again made him nauseous. Besides, he had no choice. The BJ's, as the Black Jacks had taken to calling themselves, supported him, at least on the surface. He'd best stay where he could still play. Because no matter what Oprah, Ellen, and the yammering idiots on the American Sports Network claimed about a "fresh new open mindedness," the fact remained: Nicolas Garza had likely ruined his career with his lifestyle reveal.

Which was one of the reasons he'd chosen for this ludicrous setup. Maybe he would meet the love of his life here at this exclusive resort dripping with good-looking rich guys hiding from the world. He sighed and walked into the main sitting area of the luxury suite, prepared to meet his newbie buddy for the first night.

His feet froze and his whole body contracted in response to the man who stood in the doorway, thousands of miles from Michigan, suitcase in hand, Ray Bans sliding down his patrician rich-boy, American nose.

"What are you doing here?" Parker spoke first, breaking the moment. He glanced at the number on the door and on the key card in his hand as if they held the answer. Nicco saw a drop of sweat bead up on Parker's temple. He ached to leap across the room, hold the obviously anxiety-riddled young man until he relaxed.

How this had happened, he had no idea. His heart pounded in a new rhythm, one of sweet anticipation.

Nicco stuck his hands in his pockets, determined to remain nonchalant. "This is where I was told to come, for my, ah, rookie trip."

"Well they've obviously screwed up." Parker dropped his case and frowned. Nicco's mouth went dry. "I'm here too for ...holy shit. And you're a rookie at these things?" Parker's voice cracked, which made Nicco want to laugh, and cry and run away from him all at once.

He shrugged and tried to keep his voice neutral. "Yeah, so I see. And as a matter of fact, I am a rookie at 'these sorts of things.'" He hooked fingers around the words, which felt lame and stupid.

"No. Hell no. No fucking way." Parker started to back away, but his foot tangled in his shoulder bag strap, and he landed on his ass, cursing like a sailor. Nicco burst out laughing so hard he had to sit.

Parker scrambled to his feet and frowned. Nicco kept guffawing, as the stress of the past months and the extreme surprise of seeing the object of his lust at the door overwhelmed him. Finally he shook his head, unable to suppress a wide, innocent grin that made Nicco's heart hurt all over again.

I won't do this to him. He's too good for me.

Wiping his eyes, he rose and faced the tall, handsome American, put his hands on broad shoulders, biting his lower lip to keep the spasms of uncontrollable laughter at bay. "You're right. This must be a mix-up." He put a palm to Parker's rough cheek, something he'd been dying to do for months and was surprised when the other man closed his eyes, and leaned into it for a half second. Then his eyes sprang open and he stepped away, rubbing his face as if scalded.

Nicco took a breath. "C'mon in anyway, have a drink. Relax. I'll call downstairs and get it changed." Parker's lean frame moved out to the balcony as his own body started a long, slow dance of horny he was going to have to work hard tonight to dispel with some lucky stranger. Keeping his gaze glued to the man's back, he picked up the phone and dialed the front desk.

After a thoroughly frustrating conversation Nicco figured out what he already surmised—the resort service had somehow matched them. He ambled out to the large terrace overlooking the perfect turquoise sea. Parker had fallen asleep in a lounge chair, which gave Nicco some unrestricted observation time. Before he did something rash, he put a hand on the man's knee, startling him awake.

"Let's take a walk." He turned and headed back into the condo, needing some space to sort out how to handle this. He slipped off his ruined shorts, pulled on a pair of plain ones and turned. His throat seized up at the sight before his eyes. Parker stood up, had taken off his shirt and now faced him, in utter silence.

Nicco had seen him hundreds of time like this, and more, considering they shared a locker room. The more he'd had gotten to know the younger man, the more he liked. His goal-oriented focus, drive, and talent had earned him the captain's role for the team. Natural leadership skills had shone since day one, and Nicco loved working with him to whip the team into shape on the field.

The subtle aura of vulnerability and innate shyness intoxicated him—a man used to show-offs, blow-hards, and self-aggrandizing assholes. Parker had a dry sense of humor, self-deprecating but not annoyingly so. Nicco would never forget the one moment they'd shared, that he'd engineered, which had nearly freaked the poor kid out so much he'd fallen down the steps at the in his haste to escape. Plus, that odd, near-miss in the locker room when Nicco had been within a literal second of shoving him against the wall and kissing him until they were both dizzy.

• • • •

PARKER STOOD AND STRETCHED, trying to clear the fuzziness and confusion and whatever else rolled around in his brain. His body creaked and popped as he turned, tugging his travel-wrinkled shirt over his head.

Nicco stared at him, mouth all but hanging open. Parker's face flamed in its usual fashion as he held the shirt in front of him.

His skin prickled, and his brain sent unwanted signals to the rest of his body, which began to betray him, in an obvious way, under his zipper.

Shit. I gotta get out of this. Now. This vacation is a huge mistake.

He swallowed and stepped past the man, who appeared frozen in place. "Excuse me." He snagged his bag and ducked into the half bathroom.

"You know, I've seen you," Nicco called through the door. "We share a locker room, for Christ's sake."

Parker propped his hands on the marble sink and stared into the mirror at his bloodshot eyes. His body thrummed with erotic energy. He had to put a stop to this. He should never have come here. He can't be with a man. It did not square with his goal of soccer stardom. And he definitely could not be with Nicco. Not and keep his sanity. "Yeah, well, you've done more than just see me if I'm not mistaken. That's why I'm in here. Thanks." He croaked out.

He emerged, determined to make the best of the next few hours and then catch a plane home. Nicco sprawled on the large leather couch scrolling around on his phone. Parker took a minute to study him, willing himself angry, anything to reject what his body wanted him to do.

His gaze traversed the long line of the man's dark-skinned legs, crossed at the ankle, up to his black shorts, to the bare and fit chest. He ground his teeth and held back, palms itching to plunge into his thick mane of hair, to run his tongue along the strong jaw, down to his tempting, copper-colored nipples.

"Fuck," he muttered willing his cock soft before taking a step into the room. He got caught in a mass of fabric as the wind blew a puff of warm air into the room, billowing the curtains right into his path. He batted them away and took his eyes off Nicco long enough for the man to get to his feet and stand mere inches from Parker.

He sucked in a breath. "So, let's walk." He stepped around the other man, yanked the door open, and stomped out into the hall.

The mantra played through his brain drowning out the sounds of the elevator during the awkward minutes it took for them to descend to the lobby. *I'm not this guy. I'm not this guy. I'm not...."*

He followed Nicco out, nodded at the beautiful women at the desk and kept his eyes roaming, anything but stare at the broad shoulders of the man in front of him.

You are this guy, Parker Rollings. You paid more money to attend a week at an expensive gay resort than some families make in three months. You are here to fuck men. Or to be fucked by them. Whatever. Nervous energy shot down his spine.

At that precise moment he could imagine Nicco's cock, against his ass, pressing inside his body, bringing pain and the most exquisite bite of pleasure. It made his face flame red and his breath catch in his throat.

They emerged onto the beach and shuffled along in silence. Soft, powdery sand felt good to Parker's aching feet after he slipped off his shoes, leaving them at the hut near the resort bar. He had no idea what to say, how to start, how to end, how to extract himself, or even make a pass at the guy.

Their bizarre history like a chasm between them, the easy conversations they'd had in and around the soccer venue felt so far away. Parker cursed himself and made a vow to only stay a few minutes, then get his ass back onto a plane out of here. They must have walked nearly an hour, well past the boundaries of the La Luna resort, in what had eased, somehow, into a comfortable silence.

He heard a shout. "Nicco! Nicco!" A small, dark skinned boy ran up, a gleam in his eye. "Is it you?" Nicco grinned at the kid.

"Yeah, I believe so." He shrugged at Parker who couldn't resist a matching smile.

"Hey, d'you wanna play? You and—hey, you're Rollings, aren't you? From the Black Jacks! Hey guys!" The kid ran off, leaving Parker and Nicco standing for a few seconds. Then they found themselves surrounded by a gaggle of boys and girls of all ages. A soccer ball appeared, got kicked into the air, and the race was on.

Parker grinned. This he understood.

The sun beat down on the near-paradise of sand and sea as the men jumped into the pick-up match, playing full out, giving a few tips, but mostly enjoying the beautiful game they both loved.

Parker feinted, moved past Nicco, passed and his small team scored, causing paroxysms of delight, high fives, and various celebrations. Nicco frowned, called his team in for a quick conference, then raised an eyebrow at Parker and held up a hand to signal resumption of play.

Parker trotted forward, easily maneuvering around the small bodies, letting a few of them take the ball from him on purpose as he made his way to the makeshift goal. "Now!" He heard Nicco call and suddenly the entire opposing team descended on him, circled him, forcing the ball away from his feet by the sheer mass of their numbers. He grinned, sprinted after Nicco who headed straight for the opposite end.

Before Parker reached him, he planted the ball into the small net and turned to accept his own celebrations. Parker watched, sweat dripping from his hair as the man let four or five small kids climb up his arms. Parker's chest constricted at the sight, scaring him, forcing him to turn away.

After another hour, the kids' parents gathered them up, took about a million selfies, then the two men wandered back to the La Luna private beach and sat together, sore feet stuck in the surf. Covered in sweat and sand, Parker allowed a happy relaxation to ease into his chest.

He dropped back on one elbow and watched the huge red sun-globe hover over the sea, turning the fluffy clouds an amazing array of colors. He observed Nicco rolling his shoulders and propping his elbows on his knees and wanted more than he wanted to his next breath to reach out and touch those shoulders, back, and more. He shook his head.

"That was fun." He hated the sound of his own voice.

"Yeah," Nicco grunted, keeping his gaze trained on the horizon. Frustrated fury surged through Parker's brain.

"Look, I'm sorry I've fucked up your resort weekend by showing up. I don't want it either so I'm gonna head back and see if the front desk can get me a flight." He gasped when Nicco turned to him, mocha dark eyes glistening with emotion. Within seconds the man loomed over him, hands on either side of Parker's face, forcing him to lie back or they'd knock foreheads. The other man's warm breath, his intense stare, made Parker shut his eyes, willing the urges coursing through him far, far away. Then, suddenly, he didn't want to fight it anymore.

The sand scratched his back, the cool water lapped at his feet, and when he opened his eyes ready to accept whatever Nicco offered, the man glared at him then backed away. Resuming his seated position, staring at the sea. Parker stayed put, flat on his back, collecting himself. A warm palm touched his thigh.

"I'm glad you're here. Stay. *Por favor.*"

Parker closed his eyes again, terror and raw, primal lust raging through his soul. While something else in him achieved a sort of peace then, with Nicco's light touch to his leg. This would be complicated. As he propped himself back up on his elbows and the men sat in comfortable silence for a while, he knew it would be worth it, and determined to make it so, for both of them.

Chapter Fourteen

Nicco winced as his newly-sore feet hit the cold tile of the bathroom floor. After a long hot shower, he wound a huge towel around his waist. As a small spark of anger caught, burning a little brighter behind his eyes.

Jesus Christ, Garza, you seduce men and women with ease. What is your fucking problem? You want this kid. Take him. He's obviously ready. It's a purely physical act. You understand the mechanics. The kid is an obvious bottom. You prefer to top. Perfect. Do your thing.

Nicco's chest burned and his skin felt raw, flayed at the word floating through his head about Parker..."mine." At loose ends, unsure if he should amble out of the bathroom naked, with a towel, fully dressed, or what, which pissed him off even more.

He glared into the mirror. Dragged fingers through his wet hair and set his shoulders. He'd be damned if this kid, this...unbelievable, handsome, smart, talented, and compelling man would turn him into a nervous teenager.

He jerked the door open and walked out with the large towel still around his waist, determined to get control of this thing. To take what he wanted, go back to Spain, and never darken the door of America again. Not if it meant exposure to heartbreak. He'd come out publicly, so he could never play in Europe. He had plenty of money. He could retire, consult, coach, or sit on a beach for the rest of his life. Of all the things Nicolas Garza was careless about, one of them was never money.

It had been a foolish stunt with the Black Jacks, putting himself out there, a prancing pony for the media to drool over and the public to crush to their collective, open-minded bosom—or vilify as "all that was wrong with sports." He'd cut himself off at the knees with it for certain. He was stuck in America now, of all places, the country that had at least at first taken on his open homosexuality with a media-frenzied fervor.

All the foolish fantasies he'd allowed himself years ago with Leandro, the one man he loved more than life, came rushing back. Scenes of domestic bliss, of shared goals, happiness, and more flashed through his head as he took in the sight of Parker. The tall man stood in front of a gigantic television tuned to a premiership game, shirt in his hand, his perfectly-formed back and broad shoulders an insurmountable temptation.

Nicco took a breath and headed for the mini bar. Alcohol. That would help.

Parker whooped when someone scored. "Hey, did you ever play with...."

"Yeah, probably. All of 'em at one point or another." Nicco dropped into a chair, beer in hand, letting resentment burn bright. "I'm old, remember?" Parker's eager face turned back to the screen, as he bent one leg then the other stretching out his quads and hamstrings, his lithe body moving under Nicco's gaze.

They both watched the match unfold, go into stoppage time then end on penalty kicks. By the time it ended they sat side by side on the couch, an easy familiarity between them. Without a word Parker jumped up and disappeared into the bathroom. Shower noises drowned out the final commentary from the broadcast.

Nicco flipped the television to a music channel. When Parker re-emerged dressed in a towel and nothing else, the latest R&B song drifted through the large room. Nicco walked up to the object of his desire, deciding to be as straightforward as he could.

"Look, Parker, I'm, um, not gonna kid you. I want...ah...." The expression on Parker's face stopped him. Deer in the headlights, combined with a tinge of anger and abject terror sent red flags flying all across Nicco's brain. "Never mind."

He sat back down and drained the rest of the beer. A complex array of emotions played across the young man's face. Nicco watched, amused, and then resigned. He put a hand on Parker's shoulder. "It's okay. I understand. I'd try to escape me too. I come with my own media circus now. Why would you want to subject yourself to it?"

He stood and made his way to the bar again, needing to drown, to shut out, to close off any and everything. "You should go, young Parker. You aren't safe here. Not with me." He kept his back to the man, throat hot and tight with unsaid words.

Before he could pick up his drink, strong arms encircled him. A firm chest pressed against his back. Lips found his neck, trailed down to his shoulder. The unmistakable sensation of a hard cock against his ass made him groan and raise his arms, reach behind him, grip Parker's thick hair in his fingers. "You don't want to do this," he whispered still facing away from the man he suspected he already loved.

The hands roamed across his body, down, yanked the towel away in one quick motion, leaving him bare and exposed and pulsing—heart, soul, and body.

· · · ·

PARKER HEARD NOTHING but Nicco's breathing, felt nothing but Nicco's soft, silky skin. He kissed the deep brown flesh, closed his eyes and let his hand move, taking him places he never thought he'd go. But he had to, now. He required the man's lips on his like he required oxygen to breathe.

Nicco turned slowly, held out his arms. Parker went into them, as lips, tongues and teeth clashed with urgency. Nicco's hands roamed all over him. Parker heard himself moaning, sighing Nicco's name. His brain released every ounce of tension and anxiety he'd been harboring about this very moment, the moment Parker became true to himself at last. His eyes burned but Nicco kept kissing him, muttering something around his lips as he reached down to tug Parker's towel off.

He grunted when Nicco gripped him. He trembled, confusion taking hold, making him dizzy. The hand kept up its steady rhythm, lips stayed on his, tongues met and retreated. The room dimmed around Parker's vision.

"Holy shit." His cock twitched, pulsed and released. He groaned and shook, mortified at his teenager-ish knee jerk orgasm. "God." He broke away, stepped back, his ears buzzing with shame and a low hum of still unfulfilled need. "I'm, um, sorry." He took another step away from the man who'd compelled him to act this way. Now he really needed to leave but wanted to stay, to wrap himself in the blanket that was Nicco and never emerge.

Nicco held out a hand, his gaze soft, his full lips pursed with concern. "It's okay," he soothed, putting a hand to Parker's boiling hot face. Lips touched his, gentler this time, but firm with purpose.

Parker sighed and wrapped his arms around the other man, reveling in the hard planes, the angles, and rough skin. Nicco maneuvered him backward towards the couch. They stayed standing, hands unable to settle as Parker allowed himself to touch Nicco all over.

The amazing velvet of Nicco's shaft filled Parker's hand as he palmed it. His own cock surged back to life, springing up between them.

"Let go a minute. Trust me. I need to feel you against me," Nicco murmured against his lips. Parker wound his shaking fingers in the silky depths of Nicco's hair, groaning with satisfaction as their bodies melded, heat meeting heat. Nicco broke away then, put his hands on either side of Parker's face. Parker tried his best to calm his breathing but he couldn't, didn't want to.

"Fuck me. Nicco. Please...I...want you to." Nicco blinked, took a long breath, then pressed kisses to his nose, both cheeks, his neck, making him moan and fist his hands in the long, silky hair again. "Please. God, Nicco."

"No, Parker. I can't. I won't. I'm no good for you...." Their lips met again and they dropped to the couch together even as Nicco protested.

Parker couldn't tell where he ended and Nicco began. The realization made a bright beam of happiness pierce his brain.

"Stop!" Nicco pulled away then, disentangled himself and sat, his shoulders heaving. Parker leapt to his feet, stood in front of the man who'd enticed him on so many levels. Putting a hand to his chin he tilted the dark, handsome face up. Their mutual nakedness felt completely natural. Parker's usual reticence about nudity vanished in the flash of Nicco's dark, sexy stare.

"I *won't* stop. I want this. So do you. I *will* stop pretending though. If you will." He stepped closer, his throbbing sex inches from Nicco's lips. "If you won't fuck me then...." he gasped as the other man rose, gripped his face, and stared into his soul.

"I'm not going to fuck you, Parker. But I am going to make love to you. Over and over and over again." Parker dropped his hands to his sides, let Nicco kiss him, allowed himself to accept his touch everywhere, fist his cock, drop to his knees and nearly make him pass out with the sensation of lips, tongue, and throat.

Their combined breathing rasped, loud, overpowering the music pounding from the speakers. After nearly bringing on another mind-blowing orgasm and making Parker want to cry with satisfaction, he stood, wiping his lips. "Now. To the bed." He took Parker's hand and led him into the other room. The curtains billowed around them, lending a surreal air to the lusty energy between them.

Nicco sat, tugging Parker down next to him, palmed his cheek, and kissed him long and deep, making every nerve in Parker's body sing out. He reached for Nicco's cock, needing something to touch, another connection of some sort. Nicco shifted his hips to give him more access. Their lips parted.

"That's it," he whispered into Parker's skin. "Now lie back, let me show you...." He eased him down onto the bed, kissing and licking every inch of skin.

Parker's body ached, his head pounded, and an emptiness he'd never sensed before made itself known, beating into his brain, making him feel hollowed out. He pulled Nicco's face up from its current mission lapping at his nipples. "Please. Show me."

• • • •

NICCO'S HEART FLUTTERED, his body pulsed with something he refused to name as he stood and retrieved a tube of lubrication and some condoms from his suitcase. A virgin—not something he'd encountered in a while. But this delicious man—his Parker—lay there, so ready and amazing all spread out on the bed. His bed. His Parker.

Nicco shivered, shook his head, and smiled, lying alongside the other man, running his hand down Parker's beautiful face, neck, shoulders. He leaned in for yet another mind-boggling kiss, groaning at the touch of the other man's hand on his flesh.

Go slow. Take it easy. Enjoy. It might be the only chance you get.

"Parker," he whispered. "My love, I think you're ready."

"Actually, if you don't fuck me now I'm really gonna be pissed." The breathy voice made him grin, as he eased his fingers out, as the beautiful man lying on the bed hissed, and blew out a breath.

Nicco stood, shaking and speechless, then ducked into the bathroom to wash his hands and roll a condom down his shaft. When he emerged, Parker had turned over. "No." He said, his voice hoarse. "As tempting and perfect as that is, I... I want to look at you. I need to watch your face while we make love."

• • • •

PARKER STARED AT THE ceiling as his body calmed, cradling Nicco's dark head to his shoulder, his body languid with satisfaction. After a few minutes, Parker tilted Nicco's face up and pressed lips to his.

"Don't ever leave," he whispered.

"I won't," the man sighed as he stood, threw away the condom, and hit the bathroom. He emerged, wiping his hands on a towel. "You okay?" Parker sat, wincing, and limped to the bathroom. His ass stung but his heart was full and his brain calm for the first time in years.

"I've never been more okay in my entire life." His leaned in the doorway, watching Nicco stretch out on the bed. "How is that? You are bad. I should avoid you. At least that's pretty much what everyone's told me."

Nicco's face softened. "I've been bad, yes. But now, I'm completely good. With you. Badness over." He raised a dark eyebrow. "Well, other than the badness I'm about to get into with you." Parker sighed and flopped down beside Nicco, tugging the satin duvet up to cover their naked flesh. "Roll over, lover. I need some sleep," the man whispered. He kissed Parker's shoulder, making his skin quiver. "We have a whole week. Never fear. I'll teach you a lot. But you have to promise to teach me something."

"What?" He muttered, easing into sleep, held tight in Nicco's arms. "If it's the one move where I take the ball away...."

"How in the hell I can ever stop loving you."

Parker smiled, pulled Nicco's hand to his lips. "Okay. It's a deal."

Chapter Fifteen

Parker flopped down on his leather couch, exhausted in body and mind. And lonely beyond belief. He'd spent six weeks of the off-season time traveling with Nicco, seeing places he never thought he would—Paris, Rome, Madrid. During their time away to themselves, he'd learned more about his lover than he thought possible.

Including the fact that Nicco seemed stuck in constant "go fast" mode. It wore Parker out on a certain level, irritated him when he wanted to laze around on a Sunday, watch TV, read, fuck a few more times before taking a nap as the hustle and bustle of an Italian street below floated up to their open hotel window.

"Lazing around" never seemed to figure into Nicco's daily plan. He would take time to screw around, happy to teach Parker all the fun ways they could get off together. But after the first time when Nicco had asked how he could help but love him, he seemed to be on a mission to make Parker come as many ways as possible. Not that Parker complained about it. But they never returned to the highly emotional moment, not once. Which pissed him off.

He required emotion along with the physical. One of the things he found out about himself during the admittedly fun, sexy trip was how well he slept in Nicco's arms. Of course, in the morning, after a vigorous and fully satisfying lovemaking session Nicco would literally leap out of the bed as if his skin were on fire and force Parker into a long day of sightseeing, drinking, eating, and then a full night of clubbing.

At times, Parker wondered if the man remembered he had uttered the "L" word. By the time they got home, he wondered what had made him think Nicco capable of love at all. Lust, yes. Fucking constantly, without a doubt. Capable of nonstop fun days and nights. But Parker required something more—a return to their first night. The slow, erotic, easy love they'd shared but had not returned to since.

So when they'd landed back on Michigan soil from their long vacation, sun burned, sore in intimate places, and irritable, he'd turned to Nicco in the taxi and told him he needed a break. Just a short one, so he could sort out how he felt.

Nicco had stared at him, unblinking, for over a minute, dismay in his eyes morphing into something resembling anger. Then, finally a scary neutrality masked his face, as if Parker's behavior were to be expected. As if nothing had happened between them but a whole lot of sex.

Now he sat, having spent five days ignoring the man and feeling as if he'd had something vital ripped out of his chest. He stared at the sports network, not seeing or hearing it. Picking up his phone, Parker willed Nicco to call or text, or something. Two could play at the ignoring game he guessed. He cursed and tossed the device to the floor, falling almost immediately into a deep sleep.

After the La Luna vacation, they'd decided to keep their relationship quiet as long as they could, not out of embarrassment but jealousy. They craved privacy to explore each other's bodies while being able to still function in public without photographers, admirers, and haters dogging their every step. It had worked, but entailed an annoying routine of "who stays over" and "hide the incriminating car somewhere" at both of their homes, which had led Nicco to suggest the vacation.

Tension reigned supreme around the Black Jacks headquarters, even during the off-season. After the initial supportive groundswell for Nicco's coming out, three team members had requested transfers. Nicco had had to hire a security guard for his suburban condo complex, thanks to a couple of scary brushes with vehement hate groups.

It had been a trip, a buzz, a crazy, surreal set of weeks strung together where Parker was alternately ecstatic and orgasmic, or furious with Nicco's seemingly blasé attitude about their relationship. Parker didn't get it. He simply could not imagine a way they could be together and still play pro sports, and half the time he thought Nicco didn't even care one way or another. Maddening, but dear God he missed him.

When the buzzer sounded, signaling someone on the ground floor of his building wanting in, he jerked awake, disoriented. He groaned and got up, every single bone, muscle, and sinew on fire with pain from a hard workout. Figuring it was Nicco, half glad and still half mad at him for proving such a stubborn asshole, Parker hit the entry button, then poured a huge glass of water while he waited.

Smiling when the doorbell sounded, he opened the door, something appropriately sexy and inviting on his lips. The sight of the tall, dark and angry looking Terrance made the smile fade. "Can I help you?" he asked, tugging a shirt down over his bare torso when he realized it was not Nicco on the other side of the door.

"No, but I'm going to help you," the suave-looking man said, keeping his distance outside the door.

Parker glared at him, crossed his arms, and said nothing. Terrance smiled, his teeth shining in stark contrast to the deep mocha hue of his face. "Oh...you are cute. I can see why Nicco would be smitten by you." He leaned on the doorjamb, loose-limbed, comfortable in a way Parker envied.

"I don't need your help," he said, his hand on the door, ready to slam it shut.

"Well, we'll call this an information session then. I'll tell you what I think you should know about your new boyfriend. And then you can decide what you do with it. How about it?"

Parker scoffed. "Beat it, Terry. I'm good. Nicco's good. We're together. That's all you need to know." Although, of course, they weren't together, and hadn't even exchanged a text message for days. He set his face in calm lines, trying to strike a take your jealous shit out of my house attitude.

"Hmm...." The other man smirked. Parker tried hard not to slam the door in his face. The deafening silence from Nicco in the last few days had never sounded so loud. "Not sure you realize this but," he looked down at his hands as if ashamed of what he was about to say, "Nicolas Garza is a sex addict."

Parker blinked. It sounded like something you might toss out as a joke, a half-compliment…or something painfully obvious.

His own recently neglected skin, so eager for Nicco's, burned with memory. "Yeah. And?"

"I mean, adorable little former virgin, he has a problem, a sickness. He has to get off nearly constantly and typically doesn't care how, or with whom, as long as he can come—over and over again. Surely you've noticed his…insatiability…you know, on your little vacations."

Parker shifted, nervous and angry at this asshole standing at his door, making him feel dirty, like a used condom. Defensiveness obvious in his voice, he replied, "Yeah. I did. I liked it. You can go now." But, unbidden, a fleeting memory shot across his brain. They'd gone to plenty of nightclubs, some hetero, several not. And a trip to one in Paris had resulted in their first legit argument.

Parker hadn't liked the way Nicco's eyes raked the room, scanning it constantly. Then how they'd narrow, darken as he found an attractive woman—and the place had no shortage of them. The woman would almost always be staring back at him with clear invitation shining in her eyes. Ironically, however, the argument had ensued because Parker got dragged into a scrum of ladies on the dance floor while Nicco sipped and watched, his gaze intent.

"So," Nicco had asked as they walked to their hotel in the wee hours, sweat drying on their skin, "you want to give it a try?"

Parker had stopped, put a hand on Nicco's arm, not sure what the guy meant but too tired and drunk to give a smart answer regardless. "What the fuck are you talking about?"

"I mean, sexy American boyfriend," Nicco had grinned and pulled Parker into an embrace. "I can arrange a little group fun, with some members of the less hairy sex for company. If you like." Parker recalled grinning at the sensation of his lover's erection pressing against him, making his own body respond in kind. His lips had been soft, whispering near Parker's ear. The Paris night had been warm and full of promise. He'd bitten Parker's earlobe then released him, stepping back with a confusing, angry look on his face.

Parker shook his head, remembering the whole bizarre scene. He'd said no, no thanks. Not interested in sharing you. Nicco had remained sullen the rest of the walk back. By the time they hit the hotel door, Parker's alcohol fueled fury had bubbled over.

"I mean, I guess *you* want it though, right? I'm not enough for you? You couldn't take your eyes off all the pussy in the room. Think I didn't notice?"

Nicco had made an growling sound in his throat, grabbed Parker and shoved him up against the wall of the hotel room, his huge hand on Parker's pulsing throat. The hand at his throat, moved lower as he spoke. "You are all I want. Ever." Then he'd pressed a mind-blowing kiss to Parker's lips. Parker had yanked away, holding Nicco's still cloudy-looking face in his hands.

"Don't lie to me, Nicolas. That is one thing I won't tolerate."

Nicco had looked down, then let go of him and walked toward the bathroom. He turned back, pinning Parker with a gaze full of remorse and unhappiness. Parker still leaned against the wall, his body prepared for a nice hard fuck, thanks to Nicco's flipping of his switches once again.

"I won't lie to you, Parker," he'd said. "But I warned you. I told you I would be no good for you. Maybe you should have listened." He'd shut the bathroom door behind him leaving Parker to his thoughts.

So now, staring at Terrance, absorbing his words, he blinked. The other man's smile widened. "Ah, yes, I see you understand me now. Beware, young Mr. Rollings. Nicolas Garza is never, ever satisfied with just one person for very long. He has no control over himself and never will. Just ask his wife, or me, or any number of people he's fucked and dropped."

Chapter Sixteen

Nicco sat staring at the therapist, heart pounding with desperation. The stubborn days since parting ways with Parker after the long vacation had stretched into infuriating weeks and now two lonely months had passed without any communication between them.

During which Nicco had experienced what anyone would consider a total relapse. The months he'd spent working on his inner demons, finding other things to distract him so he wouldn't seek out random and meaningless sex faded as if they'd never happened. Both he and the psychologist agreed having the physical outlet of the grueling season did help. He'd rewarded himself with the resort trip. The one where he'd finally met up with the man he loved.

Then the ensuing weeks between the amazing discovery at La Luna and their European trip. A blur of non-stop sex bordering on marathon-level as Parker discovered what he liked and didn't like, and Nicco processed just how much the man meant to him.

Since it was the off-season they weren't required to show up at the Black Jacks' training center as often, but Nicco found himself there every day, pushing his body harder and harder as he came to terms with the fact that he had, indeed found love once more. And how much the admission terrified him beyond imagining.

Almost everything about Parker Rollings charmed, amused, impressed him—and the things that did not, turned him into a raging horndog, harkening back to his much younger days. He'd even had a tough time keeping his hands off his new lover in public. So he'd concocted the long vacation, filled with opportunities for sightseeing, long beach walks, and exotic candlelit dinners for Parker, who'd never before ventured off American soil.

He had somehow ruined it, leading to the blow-off in the taxi, and the weeks of silence that now had a life of their own. While part of him understood and in a way didn't blame Parker, he still ached from loss. Although he had certainly brought it on, forcing himself to remain emotionally aloof in order to protect what remained of his heart.

Damn psychologist had made him own that as well. The past weeks working with Josh the shrink had convinced him one could possibly be *too* self-aware. Part of him longed for the good old days—the who-gives-a-shit, utterly non-introspective, completely selfish Nicco. The one who could barely spend more than thirty minutes alone.

"I think you need to acknowledge that you have no intention of ruining anyone, Nicolas," the man was saying. "Give yourself some credit. You said you loved him. I believe you. You told me you've only ever loved one other person, and you know how it feels. Is it fair to Parker to just drop him now using excuses even you don't believe?"

Nicco scowled. He hated these fucking sessions. Even though he had increased them to twice a week now and had even stayed in contact with the doc while on vacation because the intensity of his feelings for Parker frightened him so much.

He leaned forward, his need to shock Josh, to make even him give up on Nicco the bad, the naughty, the never-with-anyone-very-long, taking over. "Do you want to know what I've done these last few nights, Josh? Hmm?" Josh, who'd become a lifeline for him, whom he relied on and hated in equal measure, merely raised an eyebrow. "Yeah, so after the first night after Parker more or less dumped me in the taxi home from the airport, I pouted and got stinking drunk by myself. Then I waited for him to get over himself and call me. Now, nearly two months after he told me he needed time "to think", I give up. So for the last week or maybe even two, I don't remember, I've gone out and picked up random women and fucked them, usually in public, in alleys, in back hallways, and once on the hood of my car. Oh," he held up a finger as if remembering something good. "And then last night, I went to a gay club and spent the whole time in the back rooms. You know." He raised his own eyebrow at the young man whose facial expression had not changed. "So I'm good. I'm over him. Nicco is back to normal. Parker is safe from my influence."

"Do you get tested regularly, Nicolas?" The psychologist's low, deadly serious voice made him flinch. "Because I'm guessing you don't always remember protection. It's a fairly classic symptom of personalities like yours."

"I...." Nicco ran a hand down his face, suddenly weary beyond belief. Josh had never been so direct. "Yes, I go every six weeks. And I'm clean of all the usual stuff, including the big one. Thanks for asking. And for the record, I use condoms."

"Okay then. Now let's talk about Parker."

"I don't want to." He felt like a pouty little boy not getting his way. He wanted Parker back in his arms so badly it made every inch of his skin burn. He couldn't sleep, had no appetite, and had indeed been pulling some old-Nicco bullshit with random women and did get into an orgy in the back room of a gay bar. Getting off without gaining a single measure of satisfaction—Nicco's mojo had returned.

"You need to. Because he's probably going to want an explanation about this." Josh turned his laptop around so the screen faced him.

Nicco frowned as his brain processed the collection of images there into something he tried to understand. He, Nicco, seemed to be a fairly serious-looking clench with a woman, one of the many from these past weeks. Forgettable as they all were, as they always were.

He sought something. He'd found it once with Leandro. And then at the resort he'd found it again. But his love had rejected him. With good reason since Nicco had spent their entire vacation not-so-subtly forcing him away.

He knew damn good and well what Parker required from him—his heart. Nicco didn't think he could give it. "Well, it's not his business anymore, I guess. He's the one who wanted space to think." Nicco rolled his eyes. His heart pounded and his mouth stayed bone dry.

"You need to talk to him. Take the initiative. Call him. Sitting around waiting for him to call you is making you fall back into bad habits. After all the progress we've made, it seems pretty damn counter-productive." He glared at Nicco, his eyes dark and intense. "What do you want, Nicolas, really? Have you ever once answered that question in your own mind? Because I'm pretty sure it's not random hookups."

"Aren't you supposed to be supportive of me, young Josh? Not bossy?" Nicco looked away. "I mean I'm no expert in this head-shrinkage thing but..."

"I'm supposed to be the one you can turn to when you need to talk. But I am allowed to ask questions. What do you want, Nicco?"

Nicco jumped up, shoving his seat back. "I don't fucking know, don't you get it?" He leaned over Josh's desk. The kid just sat there, implacable, and annoyingly calm.

"I think you do. If the conversations we had while you were on vacation were any indication."

Nicco made an exasperated noise and stomped out. He'd left a lot of sessions like this, he mused, as he made his way down to the locker room. He needed to run, to kick, to bash into people. He was practically crawling out of his skin. Leaning his head against the wooden door of his locker he let himself have it—the longing, the raw, true emotion he'd been fighting for months now.

"Call him," Josh's voice floated through his brain. "Take the initiative."

He stared at his phone for a full minute. Then tossed it back into the locker. He pulled on shorts, shirt, socks, and cleats and grabbed a bag of balls from the equipment room. Action, movement, physicality, that was what he required. That and nothing more.

Chapter Seventeen

Parker sat across from his coaches, his pulse racing. He'd called this meeting to warn them he wanted a transfer, for personal reasons. The sight of them made him pause. They represented something to him he truly didn't want to leave behind. It made him even more furious with Nicco for putting him in this position. He closed his eyes against the onrush of sensation—the ugly chest-crushing jealousy taking up residence once more.

It wasn't just the photos on social media. That he could almost understand—Nicco acting out, as usual. Nicco regressing after their few months of blissful calm. Parker requested the break after all. He had actually gone out on a date himself, with the lovely and accommodating Ashley just a few weeks into the break. A flush crept up Parker's neck at the memory of the night.

"Shh...," she'd soothed when he broke down after she'd asked for the millionth time why he seemed unhappy. "It will be okay."

Parker had clutched at her. Grasping at anything that might help him forget. Before he knew it their lips had met. He'd ripped at her clothes, breathing ragged, words neither of them heard escaping their lips. And then the wonderful, soft depths of a woman's body welcomed him. They cried out together, climaxing simultaneously at the exact instant Parker acknowledged he hadn't bothered with a condom.

The next morning she'd left with a soft kiss and even softer words as she sat next to him, hand to his morning rough face. "I loved you, Parker. But I know I'm not what you want. Go to him. Just get over your damn self and go."

Just a couple of days ago he'd discovered the final piece of the puzzle. He'd opened up his web-based email for the first time since returning from the vacation eight weeks ago and stared at it, confused. Until he recalled he'd let Nicco use his computer and he'd stayed signed in to his email account.

Parker closed his eyes a split second, prepared to sign out and leave well enough alone. Nothing good ever came from reading someone else's email. When he opened them, he reached out and started scrolling through Nicco's messages.

Not much in the way of incriminating really. Some communication from agents who wanted to represent him. Black Jack daily updates they all got. The email from La Luna made his face flush.

Then he stared at what appeared to be a long chain of communication from someone named Josh. Heart pounding, he read them all, none of them overtly sexual, but Nicco obviously had some sort of relationship with the guy between the "when will I see you again's?" and "thanks for calling, I needed that's" had been exchanged even while Nicco had been with him on vacation.

He signed out of the incriminating email, opened his own and in quick succession told his agent he wanted to make a change, the sooner the better. Then sent messages to his coaches, requesting a meeting as soon as possible.

He'd made a decision in his typical all-or-nothing way, he supposed. But he wanted to give the coaching staff a heads-up before he made it official. Both men had agreed to meet with him on a Saturday morning, just a few days before the player transfer window closed.

Both Metin and Rafe had shown up with their kids. Parker stood, hands stuffed into his pockets, nervous beyond belief. He'd had no brothers or sisters but liked little kids. Enjoyed doing the fan day stuff, kicking balls around with them. The time on the beach with Nicco, when the kids had accosted them into a game he would never forget.

Rafe's son sat in a cage-like thing with soft walls, messing around with random toys. Metin's baby daughter slept in a stroller, swaddled in pink. Both men seemed so happy, content with their lives. It made Parker jealous but he gulped it back.

"So I need to find a new situation," he began, not even sure he was supposed to be having this conversation outside the hearing of his newly signed agent.

"Sorry to hear this," Metin leaned back in his chair, one hand on the sleeping infant.

"Can I ask why?" Rafe came around the desk to pick up some of the toys his boy had heaved out of the playpen.

"Personal reasons," he mumbled, looking down.

"Funny, we just had this same conversation with Nicco Garza yesterday. Can I assume we can keep one of you?"

Parker glared at Rafe. "I...I didn't know he was going to...I mean...."

"Listen, Parker, you know we support Nicco. And you should know we would support...you as well."

"It's not like that." Parker looked away, frustrated fury clouding his vision. He stood up, fists clenched. Rafe's little boy chose the moment to holler, giggle, and heave a mini-sized soccer ball a surprising distance from his play base of operations. Parker looked down at the kid and some of his tension eased.

He knelt, picked up the ball, and handed it back to him. "Training a goalie there, coach?" he asked, keeping his gaze pinned on the boy who gripped the soft edge of the playpen with one hand while reaching for Parker with the other.

"Something like that," Rafe said.

Metin cleared his throat, drawing Parker's attention back to the adults in the room. "Talk to him before you make this decision, Parker. I really think you owe it to him, to you both. While I may not understand you, it does not mean I want to break up a perfectly good team over it. Well, at least not any more than it's been broken up over it."

Parker stared at the two men, both tall, fit, former top players in their day but for various reasons unable to take their careers as far as they wanted. The Black Jacks had thrived under their leadership. Parker had learned so much from them both. His pulse raced at the realization of how much he wanted to stay.

"You guys have been great. I mean, you know, about Nicco." His face flushed.

"Well, trust me, it's not been easy. But I will tell you after an initial flurry of cancelled season tickets, I'm told sales are up, beating expectations, thanks to Nicco's willingness to be the media darling, or whipping boy, whichever side you believe." Metin shrugged then smiled at his daughter who had started making baby noises. "There was a time in my life when I would never have accepted playing with a known homosexual on my team. But I used to be a young, foolish guy. I want him on the Black Jacks. I don't care how he takes his jollies." Metin leveled a serious stare at Parker. "I want you on the Black Jacks too though, Rollings. So I suggest you and Nicco get past this ... whatever it is you're going through and come to some sort of resolution."

Rafe picked up his boy who'd started to shake the sides of his confined space and whine. "We've all seen the hater bullshit. The name-calling, the conservative talk show nonsense. I think we're past the worst of it, although if you guys...ah...." He gestured to Parker, then frowned. "If you guys decide you are a couple, which I understand is possibly the case, please let us know. We have to make sure the marketing folks don't try to make hay with it any further. I don't want any more media attention. And you men deserve your privacy. Thank God the new head of the legal department agrees with me."

Parker's face reddened at the mention of the marketing department. He and Ashley had been a known couple for a while and his little one-off with her a month ago still bugged him, ashamed he'd used her. Being the tight knit little family they were, rumors drifted back to him that she'd been seeing someone else, some higher up with the casino funding them. He also knew she'd gotten promoted and now lead the public relations department. A thankless job considering how "public" the team had been about pretty much everything.

There had been pregnant girlfriends, one shot gun wedding, a few divorces, some DUIs, bar brawls, and of course, Nicolas Garza, the official gay player. Now Parker had to decide what to do. Every molecule of his being screamed at him to go back to Nicco, to hold and kiss, to soothe and laugh and play soccer and...he looked down to find Rafe's son reaching two chubby arms at him.

Rafe laughed. "This is the most social kid on the planet. Loves to be held and charm family, friends, and strangers alike. Go ahead." He held the boy out to Parker.

Parker hesitated a half second, then took the warm bundle of slightly milky-smelling child in his arms. "Da! Da!" he bopped Parker on the head with a toy he'd been clutching, then laughed so hard when Parker pretended to be hurt. "Ba! Ba!" he pointed to the ball on the floor.

Parker picked it up and handed it to him, loving the way the kid's arms and legs kept moving. He gripped the ball screeching "Ba! Ba! Ba!" the whole time. He couldn't resist taking a sniff of the boy's soft, black hair. He looked up at Rafe.

"I'll talk to him. We'll...figure something out."

Rafe took the boy back who immediately started crying and reaching back for Parker. "Hmm...." his coach said. "If you ever wanna babysit, let me know."

Parker laughed, his heart light for the first time since he'd lain on the beach in the South of France with Nicco. Their five-day silence had stretched to weeks, then months. Months of sleepless nights, written and deleted emails. Finally, he made the decision to leave the team and run away from Nicco as far as he could get. Especially after discovering the mysterious Josh, who must be some kind of online boyfriend and who had an in depth and emotionally intimate email exchange going on with his man.

Parker squared his shoulders as he walked down the hall of towards the locker room. He may not have a hair-trigger temper like so many athletes, but he didn't shy away from confrontation. Why had he not reached out, called, made an effort to get Nicco to open up to him like he did with Josh? Because if he did what he wanted to do right now—go to Nicco and be with him without lying about it anyone—he would also be out, a gay man, a gay professional soccer player.

Finally acknowledging something about himself that may very well kill his parents, could ruin his longed for career, no longer felt quite so terrifying. Because something about holding Rafe's happy little boy made him resolved and ready to confront Nicco once and for all.

If it ended it, so be it. At least he would not have run away from it without having the final conversation and regretting that the rest of his life.

Chapter Eighteen

Parker changed into a pair of shorts and shirt, grabbed his worn cleats from the bottom of his locker, and ran out onto the field. His head spinning, his gut churning. He needed a physical outlet before having the promised discussion with Nicco.

He stopped at the top of the entrance ramp, noting another figure on the field kicking balls into the back of the far goal, over and over and over. The guy had about twenty balls lined up and went at them with no break, hauling off and planting each and every one of them into the net. Parker smiled, noting the familiar way the guy cocked one elbow just before he made contact and the particular set of the man's hips as he prepared his kick.

He'd been after Nicco about it, threatening to tie his arms to his sides to force him to stop his reflexive elbow motion. It provided a dead giveaway to a long, hard kick. Nicco had scoffed and told him not to be ridiculous. Besides, training it out of him would be like training him never to sneeze or to stop blinking.

Figuring the soccer pitch as good a place as any to make up, he ran out onto the field, right in front of Nicco and made off with the ball he had in his sights next, using the elbow as the perfect indication of the right moment to attack.

"Hey!" the Spaniard called. Then when Parker turned, still maneuvering the ball away toward the other goal, he frowned and crossed his arms. "You sure you want to do this, youngster?"

Parker held up his arms in a gesture of "why not?"

The game commenced.

The men matched up physically. Slightly taller, with surprising strength in his lean, wiry body, Nicco held an experience advantage. Parker's more compact frame could be deceiving. His stamina and cardiovascular fitness had no equal. He could run for hours and hours and not tire, so when it came to it, he wore Nicco down after about fifty minutes of non-stop one-on-one. Parker loved it, the pure physicality of his game. He knew Nicco did too.

Finally, they'd played to a three-three draw and agreed to a "golden goal"—whoever scored next, won. They squared off at midfield. Nicco took possession and Parker let him, content to chase and pounce when he'd project his next move with his funny elbow thing. He stepped around him, both men moving at full speed, breathing heavy and sweating buckets.

Planting his foot in a way that would earn him a yellow card in an actual game, he lowered his shoulder into Nicco's chest and sent the other man tumbling head over heels to the turf. During which time Parker trotted downfield and gave the ball a little tap into the net. He turned, and saw Nicco still seated, head drooping between his bent knees.

Rushing back he crouched down, hands on Nicco's shoulders, terror and shame at his blatant trip making him breathless. "Oh God, are you okay? I'm sorry, Nicco."

The man looked up, dark hair soaked, arms and legs gleaming with sweat. His chest heaved as he tried to catch a breath.

Parker sat back on his ass, facing him. "Who is Josh?" he demanded, glaring at the man who had shown him what it felt like to be truly satisfied.

Nicco did a double-take, blinked, and swallowed.

"Nicolas. Who is Josh?"

"He's...how do you know about him?" The other man's dark eyes narrowed.

"You left your email signed in on my laptop. I hadn't paid any attention to it until a couple of days ago. You guys have quite the conversation going."

Parker forced himself not to crawl the short distance between them and beg Nicco to come back into his life. He would not be sharing him, however. He required some answers. "Who is he?" he ground out, keeping his hands to himself with concerted effort.

"He's...um...I mean, it's...complicated."

"Goddamn it, Nicco." Parker gave up, grabbing Nicco's arm, loving the hard muscle tensed under his palm.

Nicco yanked himself away. "Josh is my psychologist."

Parker sense of relief made him light-headed. "Your...."

"Yeah, Parker. My shrink. The guy who keeps me from going bat shit over the fact that I'm...that I...oh hell." He got to his feet, rolled his shoulders and touched his chest where Parker had shouldered him. "Nice one. Should leave a good bruise." A beat of silence filled the space between them. "When were you going to tell me you wanted to leave the team?"

Parker got to his feet slowly, keeping his eyes on Nicco's. "I didn't know you...were seeing a psychologist. Is it the..." He felt his face redden. "The sex thing?"

Nicco jerked his chin up, his eyes darkening ominously. "Yes. It is. I have a problem. A serious problem and you don't need to be a part of it. Okay? So, are you going to answer my question or what?"

"What if I want to be? Part of it, part of you, I mean." Parker's heart hurt, his lips burned to kiss and soothe the man obviously distraught standing so close to him. "And I wanted to leave the team because I thought you...didn't...care about me. I guess. And I just couldn't be here, playing with you if you...stopped...caring."

He blushed and looked up at the ceiling of the massive arena. *Just say the word, Parker.* He looked back into Nicco's eyes and let the words tumble out. "I love you. And you stopped loving me, if you ever did. So...I needed to go."

Nicco narrowed his eyes, flashing Parker the sort of glare that shot directly to his libido. "I love you too, Parker." He kept his distance, confusing Parker with body language more about *get the fuck away from me*" than the words he had actually spoken. "But now I'm afraid you have your own set of problems." Nicco stepped back, putting even more distance between them.

Parker stared at him, the perfect V shape of his torso, the way the sweat-soaked shirt clung to his body. "Um, huh?" he tried to focus and figure out how to fix this.

"Ashley called me yesterday."

"Ashley," Parker repeated, not understanding.

"Yeah. She's pregnant. And it's not the casino boyfriend's kid. It's yours."

Parker got the sucker-punched sensation again, and this time he dropped back to his ass on the turf, head pounding. Nicco crouched in front of him, brushed a strand of sweaty hair off his forehead.

Parker gripped his wrist, yanked him close, their lips inches apart. "I want to be with you," he whispered, running a shaking hand across Nicco's rough jaw. "Ashley means nothing to me. I love you...I—"

"I know that," Nicco interrupted, softening his tone. "She told me what happened. However, the fact remains, you knocked the girl up. Therefore you now have a certain level of responsibility that may not play well if we...I mean." He rose, staring down at Parker whose legs were so wobbly he didn't even try to get back up.

Nicco held out a hand and tugged Parker to his feet. They stood close enough to kiss, but merely staring at each other. "I've thought a lot about this, Parker," Nicco said softly. "And I don't think it will work. Not that I don't love you. I do love you. A lot. But you can't afford to be entangled with me, with this whole gays in sports thing. You're going to have a kid. It won't be fair to you, or your...child." Nicco looked away.

Parker jumped to his feet and started walking away, his vision blurry with anxiety. He turned when he was halfway across the field and yelled at the top of his lungs. "I love you, Nicolas Garza. I don't give a fuck who knows about it." He pointed, his hand still shaking. "If you want to cop out, freak out and push me away, I want you to know right now it's your fault we won't be happy. I will tell the whole goddamned world how I feel about you. I don't care. I'm sick of your excuses."

Nicco started toward him, his lips settled in a tight line. Parker kept walking backward, willing Nicco to keep coming, to follow him out. When his back hit the wall of the entrance ramp leading from the pitch down to the locker rooms, they were in near complete darkness. Parker reached out, found Nicco's hand, and tugged him close. "Don't do this to us," he whispered before slanting his lips over Nicco's, groaning with relief at having the man back in his arms. "Don't."

Epilogue

Three Years Later

Nicco smiled as he turned the corner from the kitchen into the large sunny family room. He held a backpack and a small soccer ball. Ross' mother had just sent him a text to say she'd be about ten minutes late but didn't have time to come in and could they bring the boy out to her. His heart jumped into his throat at the sight of the child sitting in Parker's lap, a book open in front of them.

Parker had his chin resting on Ross's dark blond head, letting the boy turn the pages. Of all the things Nicco ever imagined himself doing, co-parenting a boisterous, energetic and scary-smart son with his lover had not been one of them. But he wouldn't trade the last few years for all the money in the world. He leaned in the doorway, watching. Then when his phone dinged with a text he remembered what he'd told Ashley.

"Hey, kid, your mom's here. She's in a hurry. Let's go. Here's your stuff."

Ross looked up and beamed at Nicco. When the boy leapt off Parker's lap and made a bee line for him, Nicco knelt, taking the warm little body in his arms, and held him close. "Uncle Nicco, I don't wanna go."

"Sure you do. Your mom needs you and so does Scott," he named Ashley's accommodating, wealthy, casino-boss husband. "And I hear your baby sister misses you so...off you go!"

Ross held him in a death grip, his arms strong for a toddler. Nicco stretched out his other arm and enfolded Parker in the group embrace. Finally Ross lifted his face from Nicco's shoulder, his impish grin back in place.

"Love you, Uncle Nicco. Love you, Daddy," he said, wiggling down to the floor and grabbing his stuff. "See you tomorrow night? At the match?"

"Yep." Parker crouched down and gripped his son's hand. "I love you too. Be good for your mom and Scott and give baby Ellie a kiss for me."

The two men stood at the door, waved to Ashley, and watched Ross clamber up into his car seat. She blew them kisses after fastening him in and sped away in her obnoxiously expensive SUV. Parker sighed and leaned into Nicco a moment. "I miss him already."

"Me too." Nicco kissed Parker's hair, then tugged him back inside. "I have an idea for some activity that could distract us, however."

· · · ·

LATER, AFTER A LONG run, then dinner, Parker lay on the leather couch, watching a Euro league match. Nicco brought in a couple of cold bottles of beer. Accepting one, he moved his feet to make room on the couch, reflecting on the tumultuous last few years with a smile.

The two men had become an acknowledged, accepted couple. They led a few low-key fundraisers for gay rights in the workplace and, of course, for same-sex marriage, which had just become legal a few months earlier. It had killed Parker that if anything happened to him and he was incapacitated, the damn owner of his team had more say over him than did his partner of the last three years. And he planned to make a change to that, tonight.

After three winning seasons no one would argue with the Black Jacks' success. The leadership remained solid. Metin and Rafe had settled into their roles as co-coaches. They had a new legal department able to ride herd on the promotions and marketing department. The fake Instagram account the marketing geniuses has set up had been shut down after getting several players in trouble as fans took it as a challenge to catch a "BJ" out misbehaving and posting it up as quickly as possible. Nicco had lain low, remaining completely out of the limelight except for his abilities on the field, which proved just as amazing the subsequent seasons as the first.

And Parker loved him. Was truly, madly, head over heels with the man. Not that they didn't have their differences of opinion. They were prone to knock-down drag-outs, leaching onto the field at times, just like any other couple who worked together, he supposed. He plopped his bare feet onto Nicco's lap and sipped his beer. Nicco changed the station to some random violent movie, leaving Parker content to drift and observe his lover's profile as he got sucked into the killing and bloodshed on the screen.

At one point, as if sensing Parker's gaze on him, Nicco glanced over, his face lighting up with a smile that made Parker's heart pound. He had continued his therapy and fully owned up to his past addictive tendencies. He fought the demons still, but Parker kept him focused, and having a baby, then a toddler around half the time kept them both near exhaustion.

Being a parent had made Parker feel complete. He adored his son and truly appreciated the boy's mother, who had so readily agreed to let him be a huge part of Ross's life.

The hand Nicco had resting on Parker's leg moved up, under the towel Parker wore after his shower. "Mmmm...." Parker sighed and slid down, shivering as his lover grasped the hard-on he'd been sporting since Nicco had come into the room. "Whatcha gonna do with it?"

Nicco shrugged, feigning boredom as he kept his gaze on the large screen, but his hand moving against Parker's flesh. "I'll think of something," he muttered.

Parker sat up, turned Nicco's dark face to his. "I love you," he said, threading his fingers in the man's silky black hair.

"I love you, Parker," Nicco said simply, as he dropped down to one knee on the floor. Parker looked at his outstretched palm. It held a heavy rings. "I want to be with you forever. Please."

Parker took it, grinned, and tugged a nearly identical one out of the side table drawer. Nicco's eyes watered as Parker slid it onto his left ring finger then let his lover do the same for him. "This is gonna cause another shitstorm, you know," he said as he pulled Nicco into his arms.

"I don't care," Nicco declared before dropping into sleep, leaving Parker to run his fingers through his hair, contemplating how much of a mess it would cause and how they'd weather it together.

• • • •

The End

IF YOU LOVE THIS STORY, then you owe it to yourself to read the first two books of the Black Jacks of Detroit series!

Be sure and get back to me and let me know what you think! They are best enjoyed in this order:

Red Card

Shut Out

This series is tied in with my best selling one, The Stewart Realty series.

It is best enjoyed in this order:

Floor Time

Sweat Equity

Closing Costs

Dual Agency

Escalation Clause

Conditional Offer

Mutual Release

Backup Offer

Good Faith (This novel is not a romance but a 2nd generation novel with plenty of romantic elements. Please read the content warnings before you start).

About Liz Crowe

. . . .

LIZ CROWE IS A KENTUCKY native and graduate of the University of Louisville living in South Carolina. She's spent her time as a three-continent expat trailing spouse, mom of three, real estate agent, brewery owner and bar manager, and is currently a digital marketing and fundraising consultant, in addition to being an award-winning author.

The Liz Crowe backlist has something for any reader seeking complex storylines with humor and complete casts of characters that will delight and linger in the imagination long after the book is finished.

Her favorite things to do when she's not scrolling social media for cute animal videos is walk her dogs, cuddle her cats, and watch her favorite sports teams while scrolling social media for cute animal videos.

Follow along with Liz online at lizcrowe.com

Sign up for her newsletter at lizcrowe.com

Follow/ like @lizcroweauthor on Facebook, Instagram, Twitter, TikTok

Don't miss out!

Visit the website below and you can sign up to receive emails whenever Liz Crowe publishes a new book. There's no charge and no obligation.

https://books2read.com/r/B-A-ZHTD-RYLED

Connecting independent readers to independent writers.